CONQUEST'S CONQUESTS

CONQUEST'S CONQUESTS

or

Socio-Political Policy In Modern Britain
As A Game Of Two Halves

A Novel By

GJ Babb

Copyright © 2024 GJ Babb

gjbabb.com

The moral right of the author has been asserted.

Apart from any fair dealing for the purposes of research or private study, or criticism or review, as permitted under the Copyright, Designs and Patents Act 1988, this publication may only be reproduced, stored or transmitted, in any form or by any means, with the prior permission in writing of the publishers, or in the case of reprographic reproduction in accordance with the terms of licences issued by the Copyright Licensing Agency. Enquiries concerning reproduction outside those terms should be sent to the publishers.

This is a work of fiction. Names, characters, businesses, places, events and incidents are either the products of the author's imagination or used in a fictitious manner. Any resemblance to actual persons, living or dead, or actual events is purely coincidental.

Troubador Publishing Ltd
Unit E2 Airfield Business Park,
Harrison Road, Market Harborough,
Leicestershire LE16 7UL
Tel: 0116 279 2299
Email: books@troubador.co.uk
Web: www.troubador.co.uk

ISBN 978 1 83628 017 0

British Library Cataloguing in Publication Data.
A catalogue record for this book is available from the British Library.

Printed and bound in Great Britain by 4edge Limited
Typeset in 10.5pt Sabon LT Pro by Troubador Publishing Ltd, Leicester, UK

Matador is an imprint of Troubador Publishing Ltd

Forging ahead in a world bewildered by the industry of bad conscience.

ACKNOWLEDGEMENT

Many things have the blame for this book. Most of all I have to thank the internet. It is the true effluvium of American culture. Its influence, in its many baleful guises, has rendered imbecilic the political class, the Press, and English institutions too numerous to mention. As such, it has been a gift to this author.

ONE

Marcus Lancing, the Labour MP for Thanet Channel, was a very modern politician. He gave the impression of being thrusting, yet familiarity suggested it was more dynamism than content. Promise had been shown from an early age. At school he succeeded indiscriminately. As a university student he was given preferment because his endorsement – as a disciple rich in indefinable promise – was flattering to those academics to whom he chose to attach himself. The specifics were a mystery to his contemporaries. There was about his progress something of prodigy to prodigal, and back again. In his rise he hardly ever applied for anything; applications for jobs and subsequent promotions were, largely, urged upon him, and rarely touched by equal opportunity considerations. Even his attachment to Labour was the gift of an early, rumbustuous girlfriend. In late middle age she was astonished to realise he was more influential and successful than any of the men for whom she had passed him over. When she thought of him a word came to mind: *pampered*.

As a local lad, Lancing went down well in Thanet Channel, a constituency only recently carved out of its neighbours by the Boundary Commission. The name was derived from the Wantsum, a channel that had once divided the Isle of Thanet from the mainland. Of strategic importance to the Romans, the channel had long since silted up and was now low-lying agricultural land. The new constituency's creation had been occasioned by the expanding urbanisation to the east on the Isle of Thanet, and to the west around Canterbury. It snaked from Reculver on the Thames Estuary to Pegwell Bay on the English Channel, spreading out from the course of the old strait.

Lancing's habitual good fortune carried him into Parliament when, for unspecified medical reasons, the severe woman favoured by the National Parliamentary Panel, and dispatched by Labour's Southwark HQ to be its candidate, cried off at the last minute. As the stand-in candidate he was handsome, modestly debonair and smiled engagingly in a way that seemed entirely wholesome. Duly elected, his diligent constituency work ensured his re-election. Without drama or noticeable effort in the House he began to be seen as quite a fixture in the ranks of Labour parliamentarians. Having established a reputation for reliability, he was uncontroversially appointed Shadow Under Secretary of State, a junior post just outside the Shadow Cabinet, concerned with the welfare of Higher Education.

Lancing's senior colleague, Jeff Deal, the Shadow Secretary of State for Higher Education took him aside to brief him. 'Look, I'll keep the government on its toes; doing the usual sabotage job. You do the blue-sky thinking.' His face took on a look of confessional gloom. 'All I see is grey clouds.'

Politicians, of whatever persuasion, joined the club of their tribe. It was an expectation that they ignored at their peril, or at least to the detriment of preferment in the ranks of their party. While honouring this convention, the politicians who were sceptical about, or congenitally indifferent to, the politics of conviction had a favourite second watering hole, the Megatherium, known colloquially as Ways & Means, situated in a grimy alley not far from St James's Palace.

Lancing was not yet a member because the sticklers on the membership committee awaited definitive proof that he brought the right degree of high seriousness to expediency. As a consequence, he lingered yet awhile in the antechamber of membership, a state he had little objection to since he knew sufficient members willing to sign him in to ensure he scarcely missed the privileges of membership. And in so doing, he saved on the monthly subscription to his personal gratification. Yet he knew that the time would come when he would have to affirm in the House his attachment to the club's principles, an eventuality that caused him little concern since, quite insensibly, he was acutely attuned to the whispering walls of Whitehall and instinctively adept at reflecting back to those he needed to impress what, in their innermost, secret beings, they wished to hear.

The Megatherium had a surprisingly grand sitting room on the first floor, which, at some point in the distant past, had been robbed from the adjacent property as a flying freehold. Originally it had been the ballroom of the London home of the *Scottish Bishops Various*, something to which, in its foppish grandeur, it ran puzzlingly counter. This peculiar provenance, and its architectural splendour, made it a fitting backdrop to intrigue and shady dealing.

This particular evening, not so very long after Covid, found Lancing lounging in the bishops' ballroom with two other MPs of his vintage, elected to Westminster as part of the Red Resistance to the Blue Resurgence. Alex Waist of East Sprawling was an old Westminster hand with previous service as an MP. He was a man of non-trenchant views who had suffered the forgivable misfortune of losing his first seat – Media City Salford – to the celebrity presenter of *Tomorrow's Politics Today*, an ingrate who had bolstered his appeal to voters by sporting a rainbow-coloured tie. Swift approval of Waist's membership to Ways & Means was a consequence of the expert way in which, at a subsequent by-election in the seat of East Sprawling, he had gone one better and stolen his Tory opponent's clothes.

'What's Thanet Channel like, anyway?' Waist asked Lancing. He was a sardonic man and intent on having a little fun at his colleague's expense, for surely his constituency was a desolation between the Isle proper and the rest of Kent.

'Dotted with villages, half medieval, half Roman,' said Lancing dreamily. 'Yeomen farmers and sheep. Staithes on the estuary and ancient saltings. Food banks in village halls and village ponds artificially aerated by local councils. Ex-coalminers in hi-tech jobs. Ninety-five percent of electricity needs supplied from renewable sources, mostly wind. Climate: wetter than Sussex, but blessed by milder winter months. Children in care: five.' He sank into a kind of stupor of satisfaction at what he had described.

Waist was at a loss to know how to proceed with his ribbing. Lancing's description was so patently panglossian it was absurd to think of ridiculing it. Once Lancing had said his goodnights and left, Waist was querulous. 'How come he has the gall to describe his constituency like that? It's the dog end of East Kent, surely?'

Lionel Partington, MP for Lower Severn, had insights. 'The Media being what it is, he fears he's on the record most of the time. He says that sort of thing to avoid controversy. His political strategy is unflinching optimism.' He wagged his head, rather in awe. 'He's a coming man; *will go far*!'

It was true; Parrtington was prescient. In the early days of his political career, Lancing had had the misfortune to be filmed by a mischievous cameraman from *Look East* who had placed him against the backdrop of Margate's graffiti-covered sea defenses. Lancing was urging the local council to clean them up for the economic betterment of the resort. At the last moment of the interview the cameraman had switched focus from him to the backdrop whereupon had been scrawled an example of the offending graffiti: *Your Mum's A Foot Fetish*. The hilarity this juxtaposition occasioned had undermined Lancing's intended message and left a deep impression. He had seen it as a warning and now was ever watchful. His skilled circumspection had consequences: he was noticed for duties even more important than those of plotting the future direction of Higher Education on behalf of the Shadow Cabinet. He was summoned to the Chief Whip's office.

'Ah, Lancing, a rather delicate matter has been passed on to me.'

The Chief Whip was a stern and unbending man in his late fifties whose connections reached far and wide.

'There's an asterisk by your name that says you're reliable. An outlier is coming in from foreign parts at the weekend. She's on a scouting trip for the was-Royals. Fiona Topp's her name. Word has come down from on high asking for someone reliable and non-controversial to handle it discreetly. Thought of you immediately. The was-Royals are coming in on a shopping trip in a fortnight's time, totally private, no press, *incognito*. Fiona Topp's a confidant, you understand, and she's going to dress rehearse the shopping, make sure the shops are operating a no customers policy, no photography, no hidden cameras in the changing rooms; that sort of thing. Can your electorate spare you this coming weekend?'

'Well, I do have a constituency surgery on Friday evening. I suppose I could come back to Town after that. Would that do?'

'It's a bit of a security detail; nothing too onerous; a courtesy. We have to be proportionate, you understand?

You were captain of rugger at your school, weren't you? Be attentive. Don't harbour any taint of republican sympathies at all?'

'*Not at all!* Royalty: a bastion of continuity, traditional values and exemplary devotion to vocation!'

'*Vocation?*' The Chief Whip seemed a bit put out. 'I think it's better expressed as *duty*. Old-fashioned ring, less careerist.'

At his constituency surgery in the old video rental store in Mistlethrush Lane, Lancing listened for half an hour to a grey, elderly man claiming National Insurance was a government inspired Ponzi scheme. Another member of his electorate wanted his wait for a hip replacement brought to an end.

'The pain is acute and constant, Minister.'

'I'm sorry, I'm not the Minister of Health, you know?'

'No, a young chap like you wouldn't be, would he? Anyway she's a woman.'

'…They're foxhunting on quad bikes…'

'…My garage was broken into last night. Third time in a month.'

'Did you report it to the police? I'm sure they would help.'

'I thought you might do it for me.'

The hotel Fiona Topp was staying at was a stone's throw from Kensington Palace and so discreet it went by its number: *Thirty-Eight*. Lancing had been expecting to escort her in taxis, but when, first thing Saturday morning, he approached the hotel he was surprised to be accosted by the chauffeur of a large, black Mercedes parked directly in front of the porticoed entrance. The chauffeur clearly knew who he was and had been waiting for him to arrive. He jerked his head in the direction of Knightsbridge.

'Sir, I'm your ride today. For the shopping.'

Lancing nodded and tried to look as if he wasn't surprised. He wondered who had supplied such luxury. It didn't look like a Labour kind of thing. Surreptitiously, he scanned the nearby buildings, wondering where the CCTV cameras were.

He met Fiona Topp in the sitting room of the hotel. She looked him up and down critically from behind dark glasses and then went back upstairs to fetch her bag. Lancing paced disconsolately, already possessed by the feeling that things were not going to go well. Visually they looked a match: smart, good-looking, urbane, but deep down Lancing could tell she was certain of things whilst he was devoid of certainty. That, he realised, was sure to lead her to think him lacking in spirit, backbone and grip.

So it proved to be. She was demanding in the high-pitched, nasal manner of entitled American femininity. 'These two guys are on off-Sloane Street,' she said, showing him a list of shops. 'You *do know* where off-Sloane Street is, *don't you?*'

They left in the Mercedes. The chauffeur was surrounded by an ominous array of electronic displays. Fiona Topp directed him where to park. As Lancing and she progressed from cult haberdashery shop to homeware store for A-listers, he could sense the distance between them growing. In a moment of chivalrous compensation he volunteered to carry the carrier bags she was accumulating. Their progress moved on to *haute couture* boutiques with wafting assistants.

'I didn't realise you were going to be doing so much *actual* shopping,' ventured Lancing as they were ushered out of a second shop. 'I thought you were just scouting for your was-Royal principals.'

'Don't be ridiculous!' she replied, stung that he had not recognised her behind her Californian shades. 'I am the was-Royal-guy-*incognito*. You're supposed to know who I am! You're the security detail guy, *dumbo*! Are you armed, *even*?'

He made a gesture that left her in no doubt he was not.

'Somebody should have told you martial arts are useless against the guys we're up against!' she said in disgust.

They parted company when the Mercedes was burdened by the biggest collection of carrier bags Lancing had ever seen. There was not one plastic bag amongst them; most had cord handles that slipped through the fingers like hanks of silk.

'Yeah, well,' she said, looking at him critically from the top step of *Thirty-Eight*, 'next time I'll bring my husband. He's got different taste to you. I hear you're in parliament. Is that fun, or is it like being a senator?'

'Well, it *is* public service, *you know*?'

'*Public service!*' She was so incredulous she pulled her shades down to the end of her nose so she could examine him over them. When she laughed it made an impression. Her laughter was almost sweet and innocent.

The next time Lancing was in the House the Chief Whip informed him, in passing, out of the corner of his mouth, 'You were a big hit! Well done. Keep it under your hat but they may be back for Royal Ascot.'

He made it sound very clandestine.

'She said I should be armed.'

'*No can do!* Would some martial arts training make you feel more comfortable? We could requisition.'

'I say,' said one toothless grandee to another as they supped on their *Cornetto Classicos* on the River Terrace, 'that young Marcus Lancing is a serious sort of chap, isn't he?

Sort you can trust with something that requires discretion. There's something about him that says *meritocracy* through and through.'

'Yes, sincere in a way that doesn't get people's backs up. Takes an interest in universities. Very grown up! I heard he's co-opted that thruster Conquest from University London Central. Wise move. Conquest's been developing new thoughts about our university system. I understand he's written a book that's going to give the government one in the eye. Formidable team Lancing's building. Could go far.'

TWO

Lancing applied himself assiduously to his political responsibilities. He had formed an advisory committee (or 'focus group', as he preferred to call it) to help him fulfill his obligations to the Shadow Cabinet. The committee met every six weeks or so. Brendan Glendale, Lancing's energetic Chief Parliamentary Researcher, drafted papers for it, reflecting his own views, which were carefully consonant with those prevailing in the higher reaches of the party. The committee's members were drawn from those with a vested interest in the future of Higher Education and who believed those interests would be best served by Labour in power. There were several Left-leaning MPs drawn from the ranks of university lecturers, an industrialist who had sponsored a science park, another who had a digital city named after him at one of the lesser universities and Professor Clifford Conquest, Vice-Chancellor of University London Central. The latter was only recently added to the committee's membership at the urging of the influential Labour peer, Lord N'Garbi.

At the second meeting Conquest attended, he unexpectedly and persuasively spoke of *disinterestedness*, something Lancing, in a moment of visionary inspiration, saw it was important that politicians demonstrated in their dealings. He caught Conquest on the stairs as he was leaving.

'I say,' Lancing called after the retreating back, '*Professor Conquest!*'

Conquest stopped and turned back a little awkwardly, marooned in the middle of the broad staircase.

Lancing hurried down to join him. 'I know we haven't had much of a chance to talk, you and I,' he said winningly, 'but I thought your sentiments on atonement were just what was needed.'

Conquest looked at the fresh-faced, somewhat young man with an expression of puzzlement. '*Atonement*, did you say?' He hesitated over the word, feeling suddenly shifty, as though he was being brought to book. 'Why? Did I sound apologetic… *regretful*?'

The other man replayed what he had just said. 'I'm awfully sorry, did I say *atonement*? I meant *disinterestedness*.'

Conquest's perplexity deepened. 'They're nothing alike.'

'I know, *most peculiar*! I think I must have had a senior moment.'

Conquest found Lancing's estimation of himself as entitled to a senior moment vaguely comic. 'You're not old enough to use that excuse,' he laughed.

'Regrettably,' agreed Lancing, somewhat deflated, 'it's one of those unaccountable things that happens from time to time.' For a moment he looked stricken. 'One dreads the possibility it will happen on air, talking to the media.'

Conquest made an effort to show he sympathised. 'I can imagine it would be concerning, but I'm afraid I've never been in that sort of situation.'

'No, and I suppose you're more of a public speaker than I… But more to the point I wanted to ask your advice.'

'About *disinterestedness*?'

'No, no, something entirely more concrete. I was wondering,' he ventured, 'whether we might discuss it over dinner?'

'Yes, of course. I'd be delighted.'

'Great!' said Lancing. 'I'll have my office suggest some dates.'

As Conquest left the building he was still fretting about how atonement had worked its way into their exchange. The ease with which Lancing had dismissed it struck him as indicative of a certain shallowness. He, on the other hand, thought the occurrence was a symptom of the psychic dislocations he detected everywhere; in the language of sports commentators, the punning of newspaper headlines and the silence of electric cars.

THREE

It might be said things were going well for Marcus Lancing, but several days later he was visited, unannounced, in his House of Commons office, by a spectral man who flashed impressive-looking credentials at him as he took a seat.

'I have to inform you that active, credible threats are circulating in chat rooms.'

Lancing shifted uncomfortably. 'Active, credible threats? What chat rooms? *Why?*'

'Royalist sympathies. You're listed with several other MPs,' said the spectre.

'I see,' said Lancing, slowly and carefully. 'Can I see these threats?'

The man pushed an envelop across the table. Inside were several sheets of A4. They were covered with line after line of black horizontal bars. 'They've been redacted as hate speech,' said the man apologetically.

'I see,' said Lancing again, even more carefully than before. He was used to a fair bit of crank mail, but threats against him circulating on-line was something new. 'So I can't see what's been said?'

'I'm at liberty to tell you the word "eliminated" is being used.'

'But surely I should—'

The man leaned forward, ever more apologetic. 'Regrettably, you don't have the appropriate level of clearance at the moment.' The red tape clearly troubled him.

'It's something we're trying to put right. I'm here to give you a heads-up, that's all. You need to be cautious about your recreational activities, your travel on public transport and use of the non-regulated public sphere.'

'Isn't that everything, everywhere?'

The spectre rose to his feet. 'We try to be proportionate. I could issue you with one of our Little Sentinel personal alarms but, things being what they are, help would come too late. There's others in the same boat, at least.' He smiled encouragingly, but the smile was wintery. 'Your name's on a watch list, and we'll be monitoring for code red traffic.'

'Isn't it code red already?'

'Lord no! Death threats are fairly run of the mill these days. After all, they're not threatening to force-feed you to your mother.' He laughed grimly, as though contemplating threats much worse. 'Those provisos I mentioned aside, carry on as normal is my best advice.'

FOUR

Vice-Chancellor Clifford Conquest spent his weekday nights in his *pied à terre* behind Butler's Wharf. The apartment building, a converted Victorian warehouse, was a short distance downstream from London Bridge station. University London Central rented the flat for him as part of the package he had negotiated when he was parachuted in to put its mismanagement to rights. His official domicile was 110 Berenson Road in Wolverhampton, which he shared with his wife, Marj, when she wasn't off on field trips hunting the fossils of ancient invertebrate sea creatures, or at international conferences discussing them. Berenson Road counted three doctors, two solicitors and a Church of England vicar amongst its residents. Conquest was not sure of the occupations of those living in his building behind Butler's Wharf, but the police had been called twice in the past year to inspect suspicious packages found in the communal waste disposal. They had been taken away without comment from the authorities, but the secrecy, if that's what it was, was unsettling.

Although it was quite a distance to University London Central's campus, it was perfectly possible for Conquest to make his way there on foot should he be so inclined. It was a matter of walking up river as far as Tate Modern and crossing by the millennium footbridge. That particular morning, the day following Marcus Lancing's focus group meeting, Conquest was enthused by the brightness of the sky and the pleasures of a leisurely walk. It was examination time and when he reached the campus it was still too early for the daily influx of students. Nevertheless, he found himself confronted by a callow, unkempt creature with the look of a student-anarchist about him.

'Excuse me, do you work for the university?' the youth demanded, fixing him with a hungry eye.

'No, I'm sorry, I don't.'

Conquest's reply could not have been more categorical. The creature looked him up and down disbelievingly, gave a wordless cry and abandoned him to seek some other source of information. Conquest walked on, telling himself that his lie had been occasioned by the type of street entanglement best avoided at all costs. Yet he felt a pang of anguish. Deep down he knew that fending off the man had deeper significance; he had shrunk with fear at his approach. After twenty or so paces he looked back and saw the man was questioning a woman he vaguely recognised as working in some departmental office. She was pointing the man in the direction of the Students' Union building. Wasn't it more likely, he thought, that he had denied any connection with University London Central because the way he managed it was grounds for strangers to target him for unspecified retribution? *No!* The whole episode was nothing more than happenstance; he was embroidering again. After all, calls for industrial action by junior lecturers about their conditions of employment and loss of pension rights were insufficient cause for threats to his person. Or were they?

He noticed a sign at the front of a nearby flowerbed. It said, 'Don't Eat The Daffodils'. It was June and the bed was populated by the usual mid-summer bedding plants. The sign, he suspected, was a witticism perpetrated by some malcontent in the Estates Department intended to make the university's risk assessment protocols look ludicrous. It was probably from the same source as the previous year's scare story about the campus being 'infiltrated' by super-ants. It crossed his mind that when he walked to work in future he should dress down. He only dismissed the idea when he realised that to be consistent he'd have to do the same whenever he ventured anywhere on the campus.

Having thus tortured himself with introspection almost to the security of the Vice-Chancellor's suite in Keynes House, he decided, *inter alia,* after all, *it's a game of two halves.*

FIVE

However unnerving Marcus Lancing might find it to be a target of on-line threats, he maintained his long-established routine of dropping in on the *habitués* of the White Hart when he arrived in his constituency for the weekend. It was safe enough, being a watering hole frequented by amiable party stalwarts who understood he was not to be bothered with the footling concerns that bedevilled his constituency surgeries. What he was more than willing to do was gossip about the latest political manoeuvring at party headquarters. His companions at the bar were wise men who believed politics was a game of two halves, and Lancing was their smart, young representative who would deliver handsomely in time. In any case, his constituency was, if not the utopia he reported it to be, on the whole well satisfied with itself.

The aforementioned were conditions when things were normal, but things were far from normal this particular June evening. As he entered the bar, having only taken the time since his arrival to change from his dark blue suit into his tweeds, he sensed the atmosphere was off. It was Mr Foreshore, who taught geography at the local comprehensive, who spoke first.

'Hello, Marcus. There's been a break-in at the constituency office. I'm afraid there's trouble brewing!'

'What's happened?' said a concerned Lancing.

'*Poodle-ism!*' said Tom Tudor, the local representative of the Environment Agency.

'*Poodle-ism?*'

'Yes, they've daubed it in big letters all over the walls!' chimed in district nurse Miriam Dreadfold.

It was true. The front door of the constituency office, which was a flimsy affair, had been burst open with ease. Now a padlock was newly attached. The walls of the main room had 'POODLE-ISM' painted on them in the gigantic, jagged lettering beloved of the inexpert graffitist. Lancing and the local committee members who had accompanied him from the White Hart stood for some time staring at the affront.

'Somebody's gone and fingered you as neo-Blairite.'

'I'm sorry? *Neo-Blairite?* For goodness sake! I'm not certain that's what this refers to! And surely we're over Blair?'

They pondered a while longer. Much though Lancing wished to dismiss it, the warning from the security officer was on his mind. He was fearful that to mention it would give substance to a creeping sense of danger. 'Unless,' he said reluctantly, 'it's some tommyrot about me having Royalist sympathies.'

'Royalist sympathies? That's hardly a crime, is it?' said the district nurse.

'It's the vicar at All Saints,' said Bill Ashford, the only Labour activist estate agent south of the Wash.

All Saints was the church that Lancing didn't attend when in his constituency. The congregation was small and prone to Tory sympathies.

'He's been sounding off again about Blair being put up before the War Crimes Tribunal in The Hague. He's inciting his parishioners against Blair in particular and Roman Catholics in general. *Now this!*'

'Yes,' said Lancing, determined to remain calm, 'but what is *this?*'

'The atmosphere's gone febrile,' decided the geography master darkly. 'There was a sixth form debate at school about after-school supervision. The anarcho-syndicalists won hands down.'

Tudor tut-tutted. 'That sort of thing shouldn't be happening in East Kent. Who's fostering that kind of stuff?'

'It's the internet.'

'Ah, *the internet*!'

They all bobbed their heads in unison.

'Well, we've reported this vandalism to the police. They came from Deal with a dog team to search for evidence, but apart from that...' Tudor shrugged hopelessly. 'I suggest you report it to someone at Westminster when you get back there. Whether it's Blair or Royalty, maybe your security needs upping.'

Lancing spent the weekend helping to put the constituency office back to rights. Two coats of paint still didn't quite obliterate the graffiti, but posters borrowed from the school extolling the benefits of scientific land management were strategically placed to complete the restoration.

His chief assistant on both days was Fay Ashfield, a slim, trim, thirty-year old who looked at him with soulful eyes when he was preoccupied by whatever task called for his attention. The moment his attention was turned on her she bashfully scrutinised her shoes. When, late on Sunday afternoon, they had washed the rollers, put the leftover paint in the cabinet in the back kitchen and cleared up, Lancing said, 'I feel like a stiff walk to clear the cobwebs. How about you?'

She nodded with a studied equanimity that belied a fast-beating heart. They took the lane to the church, crossed the churchyard, skirted a sports field where youths were playing football and found themselves in open fields overlooking low-lying countryside to the south-east, riparian land crisscrossed with ditches, all that remained of the channel that had once divided the Isle of Thanet from the mainland. Lancing looked back and saw that the dog walker he had first seen when they were crossing the sports field had followed them. He was stockstill, a silhouette at a distance, apparently gazing at something off to their left. They walked on and when Lancing turned again the man and his dog were looking in the other direction, a pointed study in indifference to their presence. Lancing said nothing but had no doubt an agent of the forces that had desecrated the constituency office was following them. He wondered whether the man could be the vicar of All Saints.

'I think you're very brave to put yourself in the firing line,' ventured Fay earnestly. 'It's very important work you're doing and we're all terribly grateful.' She had a moment of prescience. '*You've been noticed*,' she said, giving him a meaningful look at which her face, for a moment, took on an ecstatic glow.

He looked at her, glanced back at the dog walker and had that feeling that bothered him from time to time of everything being slightly out of kilter. He couldn't put a name to it; he wasn't the kind of man to make such a conscious calculation but here was hero worship of a sort. The wish that came to mind was that Vivien, his wife, would sometimes say as much. He readily conceded she was far more of an asset than Fay and her charming compliments. If only she would accompany him to his constituency more often! But she was a London socialite through and through, who had, in private, when inconvenienced by his divided loyalties between her and his constituents, referred to them as, 'Your bog people, darling'.

Back in London, Lancing went to see the Chief Whip who seemed thoroughly appraised of the new outbreak of threats. 'Yes, it's shocking what upsets people these days. Look, Lancing, my advice is treat it as a badge of honour. It means you're making a mark. Think of it as widening participation in local politics. Those in a position to offer preferment notice such things.'

SIX

Another day, another problem, thought Vice-Chancellor Conquest, except it wasn't another day, it was barely an hour since the last intractable issue had been left with him. Given the burdens of his role, he reminded himself, he couldn't be expected to do any more than surf the evanescence. As usual, it was a human resources matter and he decided – it was a bit more than a momentary thing – he didn't much care for humans.

Professor Spirakis, the head of the Department of Comparative Epistemology, gazed at him bleakly from the other side of the desk. 'Recently,' he began, 'my students, in the department's Board of Studies, expressed the view – thank you for agreeing to see me, by the way – that there is an overwhelming orthodoxy in the department in the teaching of the politics of Involuntary Human Transactional Theory.' He now fixed the nails of his left hand with a meditative stare. 'This is something, *you understand*—' he glanced up from the nails – 'on which I am no great expert, but I am aware that a certain way of thinking about this matter has *indeed* become something of an orthodoxy amongst my younger staff. I discover, on further enquiries, that in several recent conferences this adherence has been given concrete acknowledgement as the Dresden School.'

'And that's a problem?'

'It wouldn't be if my older – shall we say *more conservative* – members of staff weren't adamant that politics has no place whatsoever in Involuntary Human Transactional Theory. They regard it as an inappropriate use of the socio-economic toolbox on a rather nebulous subset of psychological theory.'

'So, it's a generational thing?'

'I wouldn't put it like that... but yes!'

Conquest was sufficiently intrigued to attempt to unravel for himself the implications of what Professor Spirakis was saying. 'And now the student representatives on your department's Board of Studies are demanding a broader account of the political dynamics inherent in Involuntary Human Transactional Theory than the one provided by this so-called Dresden School. But what they *don't want* is an account of Involuntary Human Transactional Theory which denies its openness to political influence?'

'*Exactly!* The students regard the Dresden School's approach as overly prescriptive; an issue consequential on the values of an unspoken *protestant* mindset. They are asking – *in the name of academic freedom* – for a more various account of the topic.' At this point he fidgeted in his seat, hesitating as if uncertain how much further he should go.

'So, there's nobody in the department able to teach, with ideological conviction, the alternative account the students want. *Is that right?*'

Professor Spirakis had taken on a shifty look. It was clear to Conquest that he was unhappy about the propriety of what he was doing, it being akin to washing his department's dirty linen in public at a cost to his own dignity. 'This is causing considerable disquiet. My staff – those who are seen as adherents of the Dresden School – are quite upset. They object to the idea that they are an orthodoxy. It's an affront to *their* stance on academic freedom. The fact is—' his tone had become confessional, almost pitiable – 'not so long ago the adherents were radical outliers and rather resent that they, as proponents of the Dresden School worldview, are now typified as mainstream. Before they were identified as such there was a senior professor in the department – Professor Linkage – whose views on the politics of Involuntary Human Transactional Theory were significantly other to theirs. In partnership with a Professor Richter he had been the co-founder of the so-called Zeeland Faction. They championed an account of the phenomenon that was, I'm afraid, thought lacking in the rigorous methodology of the Dresden School's approach. In fact, it was rather laughed out of consideration. It had, if you follow me, certain *catholic* characteristics.'

'And Professor Linkage...? I seem to think he's no longer with us.'

'Yes, you see as far as he was concerned there was a rather fortunate turn of events. An American university offered him a research residency paid for by a philanthropic society based in Milwaukee. It allowed him to complete the book he'd long been unable to finish whilst here because of his other duties.'

'Other duties *here*? That was rather unfortunate, wasn't it?'

'I know; he was very devoted to teaching. To be frank, his position over the politics of Involuntary Human Transactional Theory meant he became somewhat isolated in the department. These young Turks being what they are, I'm sure you can appreciate...'

'Yes, yes, there was an intellectual vogue and the younger staff pushed him aside.'

'I wouldn't quite put it like that, *but yes*. The point is, Professor Linkage's book has been a tremendous success, fundamentally challenging the linguistic and hermeneutic underpinnings of the terrain as envisaged in the Dresden School's account. And is, by-the-by, seen in some quarters as a coruscating *exposé* of the anti-libertarian instinct of the *Nouvelle* Left as it pertains to the political implications inherent in Involuntary Human Transactional Theory. And now the students are demanding the Zeeland Faction's account is given appropriate prominence in the curriculum.'

'But didn't Linkage *retire?*'

'Well yes, the year before you joined the university... he never returned from his sabbatical.'

'I see.' Conquest looked regretful but unable to help. He was beginning to find the conversation tiresome. This was an ideological matter and he considered himself at a level of seniority quite above ideology. 'Look,' he said, 'you're really rather stuck, aren't you? You've no slack in your department's establishment. Until somebody leaves you don't have a post.'

'But *we did* make Linkage an emeritus professor when he retired,' Spirakis ventured.

'Perhaps it's a pity, given the success of his research, he wasn't persuaded to return!' observed Conquest with some asperity. 'The point is, the students can't have everything they want, although it was remiss of your predecessors to allow this orthodoxy to develop.'

'I appreciate all that, Vice-Chancellor, but Professor Linkage is apparently willing to provide an account of his theories on a *gratis* basis.' His voice had taken on something of a wheedling tone. 'This is why I've brought the matter to you.'

'You mean simply as a guest of the university?'

'Indeed. He claims he wouldn't want, or need, any form of remuneration.'

Conquest was startled. 'That sounds very generous!' He paused for thought. 'I'm not sure about the protocol. It might be possible... if it solves your problem; I really can't say. Human Resources would have to be consulted... *but* since he's an emeritus professor I suspect they'll not object, provided it's short term. So... provided HR clears it, what you want is for *me* to issue him with a formal invitation on behalf of the university?'

'Yes, Vice-Chancellor, I think that would be the most appropriate way forward.'

'Then fine, I'll see to it.'

When he had gone Conquest called in his PA, Erma Radisch, and gave her instructions to adapt one of his standard letters of invitation to be sent to Professor Linkage via HR.

'And Erma,' he said as she was leaving the room, 'could you get me a copy of Professor Linkage's book. It's called *The First And The Last: A Socio-Anthropological Study Of The Unspoken.*'

SEVEN

Daniel Linkage lived above a bar of his own making. He had bought the building, very rundown, because he liked the area. True, buses trundled past day and night, but the side streets were full of the sort of apartments where young people lived and there was a station round the corner that went straight into Liverpool Street. He had modelled his bar on one in Maastricht of which he had fond memories and called it *Tatti*. He made sure the coffee was good. There were posters for Sadler's Wells next to a photograph of the Arsenal Invincibles from 2004, and on another wall photographs of Twiggy by Donovan, Duffy and Lategan. He played Bach and Mozart in the AM and jazz in the PM. In short it was civilised in the understated way of the Dutch, and made anyone from round the corner feel at home as long as they didn't want kebabs and cheezy fries. He served a *plat du jour* made by Margaret, who came every day from nine thirty until two thirty and made good on his insistence that less was more as long as you used the best ingredients, 'But nothing exotic, eh, girl?' And there was always a vegan alternative to serve the radical brethren of the Left.

Yvonne made *tortilla* at home and brought in two every day. They were gone by three o'clock when Lucy arrived. She was very decorative and knew all kinds of things about the local area. She could get you a plumber in an emergency and a course of antibiotics without a prescription. By six it was busy as hell as the trains unloaded their human cargoes from the City. Peter and Tony came in to make cocktails. Linkage turned up the volume and played dominoes with a friend until the rush passed. At ten thirty he stood on the pavement and watched the world go by while he smoked his first and last cigarette of the day. And then he closed up for the night before the rowdy boys got chucked out of nearby hostelries.

Linkage had put *Tatti* together in a handmade, fairly obvious way that should have meant it was nothing special, but nonetheless it had a stamp to it that was quite rare in all those endless stretches running northwards from the City. When he had bought the building the flat upstairs had been a wreck. Since then several builders had made an attempt to put things to rights. It still had a make-do-and-mend feel about it which was mainly because he would never wholly give over the place to the tradesmen he employed. The plumbing worked but there wasn't a matching set of porcelain in the bathroom. And neither were the kitchen cabinets a set, and they weren't from Ikea. The fact was that any workman he employed was prevented from having a clear field of action by the great many books he assiduously collected, both from posh antiquarian bookshops in places like Petworth and Hay-on-Wye, and from the local charity bazaars. The latter were, he had discovered, a fruitful source of obscure academic texts with frontispiece dedications that revealed they came from the libraries of recently deceased members of the academic fraternity.

He was a connoisseur of the way TV pundits speaking from home presented themselves. Some made a grotesque hash of it but most had the wit to reinforce their authority by placing themselves before bookshelves that were tidy affirmations of scholarship and worldliness. It was his habit to pause their disquisitions and note the titles of their books, to grade these and the other details of their self-staging in support of his disregard for their opinions. Despite this pastime, his own bookshelves were a mess; a state not entirely surprising since he was learned in the way of his library. His mind had always been too much of a ragbag to keep him to the point until it was nearly too late. The charitable might say he had deployed his learning as an extended exercise in interdisciplinarity. He had literary style and built arguments that charmed by veering here and there like a Deliveroo lad in a hurry. He saw a kind of poetry in the well-argued, although he didn't suffer gladly the species of poet that was drawn to his bar. At least he was well versed in reining in his claims to what was difficult to dispute. Having finally come to recognise all this as a weakness, he had written off his career as an academic as semi-successful. *But,* at the last, having come to understand the difference between the knowing trespass and amateurishness, and by combining rigour with the centrifugal tendencies of intellectual fashion, he had written his subtle, serpentine and ultimately lyrical defence of the politics of Involuntary Human Transactional Theory and the wider implications of the Zeeland Tendency's worldview, entitled: *The First And The Last: A Socio-Anthropological Study Of The Unspoken.* Sustained over six hundred pages by, it must be admitted, certain chemical assists, his exposition of the difficult and challenging terrain was seen, amongst other things, to have opened new doors on the dynamic nature of pre-language-based human perceptual traits. Now he was drawing his pension it caused him wry amusement to think that he was more respected as an authority in his field than he had ever been.

As a means of structuring his life, *Tatti* was more to his liking than academia. Were he inclined to contentment, he would, for the first time, have been contented. *Tatti* fixed in the neighborhood someone who was never at ease with being a local. He wasn't a nomad exactly, but he suffered the discomfort of the displaced. He had a rather brutal sense of self-worth that he concealed behind a façade of social vagueness. It had worked well with students and did now with his employees. As is the case with many a successful entrepreneur in the catering world he had created something that those who worked for him felt strongly attached to, and their engagement meant that the enterprise ran smoothly with no more than an occasional steer from him. True, he was generous in return and, as a consequence, *Tatti* was not as profitable as it might otherwise have been. As with his other savings, he had ploughed his retirement lump sum into the enterprise, but still had a hefty mortgage to service and he rented out a room to help with the monthly installments. His finances were not helped by his reputation as a generous contributor to causes of a radical, anti-authoritarian nature; the kind that led to civil disobedience, inconvenience to law-abiding commuters, and rowdy confrontations with the police. His life had taken on a certain sufficiency and he regularly declined invitations to speak on the significance of his book and the politics of Involuntary Human Transactional Theory at conferences in far-flung places. Then, there occurred, late one evening, outside a restaurant, a chance meeting with an ex-colleague from University London Central. And it was the exuberance of this occasion that eventually led to Dr Daniel Linkage, Professor Emeritus, receiving a courteous letter from Professor Conquest, Vice-Chancellor of the university, inviting him to share his thoughts on the politics of Involuntary Human Transactional Theory with the students of the Department of Comparative Epistemology. He studied the invitation over a cup of coffee that sat on a copy of the previous day's *Metro,* covering another of the punning headlines he collected. Across the kitchen, dressed in pants and a teeshirt that said *I'm a Teenage Psycho,* Max, his current tenant, was juicing oranges. Linkage had no objection to her being in his kitchen half naked since she had the legs of a thoroughbred. She was no longer a teenager either. Even so, there was a thirty-nine year difference in their ages, and his strictly-maintained fatherly concern for her wellbeing had an erotic component enjoyed by him and unacknowledged by her. He may have had a disregard for what he considered as the dismal rules of the nine-to-five crowd, but he considered himself to be a man of principle and right-thinking in all matters.

'It's really difficult to pour the juice out of this thing without spilling,' said Max without turning round.

Linkage looked at his watch. 'In half an hour you could get one downstairs without the fuss.'

'Then I'd have to pay. Your mark-up on oranges is beyond the means of a student living on loans,' she observed.

'If this is another prelude to asking for a rent rebate, it's no go.'

This was something of a running tease, because she had never asked for a rent reduction and he also forbade her to contribute to the household expenses. The fact was, he loved her being around. Her eating was the very soul of delicacy, so discerning her appetite, her company at meals adding salt to his day. Now she came across the kitchen holding two glasses of orange juice and sat down opposite him, skinny and fulsome.

She nodded at the letter he was holding. 'Presumptuous letterhead. That looks official.'

'They want me to re-visit my despicable past and give lectures. I thought it might be fun, but now I've been formally invited I'm having second thoughts.'

'*Yes!* And the students will give you the *fun-goo!*' She jabbed the sky with her middle finger. 'You have been warned!'

'I shall go and test the water,' said he with the veiled look of a conspirator, 'and only agree to exercise my addled intelligence should the auspices be favorable.'

EIGHT

Vice-Chancellor Conquest and Marcus Lancing MP were comfortably ensconced in the upstairs room of a discrete restaurant not far from Parliament Square.

'One of my researchers tells me,' said Lancing, 'that you've a book about to be published.'

'Yes, hopefully a timely if modest contribution to the debate on the future of Higher Education.'

'Not what I hear! It's said some of the more entrenched universities won't like it. I suppose you're promoting policies.'

'Well, I hope that can be said of it.'

'*Good for you!* Although one has to be cautious about policies; they can be contentious, even disapproved of.'

'I suppose that's possible.'

'What's it called?'

'Rather a mouthful, I'm afraid. *A Plan For The New University: A Vision For Higher Education Fit For Today And Tomorrow.*'

'Excellent! You must let me have an advanced copy. I'll get my staff to order enough for everyone in our focus group. Will it be ready in time for our next meeting?'

I'm not sure, I'd have to check.'

'*Never mind!* When it's ready it'll be just the sort of thing to give our deliberations some backbone.'

'Well, that might be slightly…' Conquest came to a momentary halt. 'Let's say I hope it'll be a useful contribution to the debate. I feel universities would benefit from a bit of a shake-up, I suppose.'

'Don't we all, Cliff, *don't we all*!' Lancing braced himself with a draught from his glass of Sancerre and leaned closer, wanting to unburden himself. 'The fact is, Cliff, we're not happy bunnies.'

'*Oh?* We're not? Why?'

'I seem to attract people with violent objections to what they think I stand for... which is all nonsense, by the way.'

Conquest felt a sense of comradeship. Had he not been recently prey to similar feelings of peril on his own campus? 'I sorry to hear that,' he commiserated. 'Are you in danger?'

'As time goes by, *yes!*'

'I'm rather shocked!'

'We're both trying to do good by getting on, are we not? It's a bad business if you can't be positive about things without attracting threats, even about the things you don't actually feel passionate about.' Lancing leaned forward earnestly. 'One doesn't want to be caught out by one's past, does one? That's why I think it best to avoid policies and be memorable without being meaningful.'

'Do you have specific kinds of memorable meaninglessness in mind?'

'Oh, yes. The heterogenic is better than the homologous; the primitive is modern sophistication *par excellence*.' For a moment he looked vaguely weepy. '*Any good?*'

'Well,' said Conquest, uncertain how to respond, but sensing the moment required him to say something wise and encouraging, 'I find a resort to technical niceties, using obtuse terms and the odd Latin phrase tends to baffle most people. It sounds learned, and people respect that and consider one *'above the fray'*, as it were.'

'Yes, above the fray. Y-e-s.' Lancing looked doubtful, but maybe a touch grateful for the advice too. 'One must be active and my *forte* is putting up topics to see what people – my constituents – think of them. I like to prime the gun, without actually shooting anyone... or anything.' A blankness stole over his face, suggesting he was already moving on to some other worrisome topic.

'What,' Conquest wondered, 'are the sort of things you find people object to?'

'*Poodle-ism.*'

'Ah!' As far as Conquest was concerned there was some justification for that particular jibe. 'Weren't you once a Blairite babe?'

'No, I was *not*! I got my tradecraft at the bar.'

'Really? *The Law?*'

'No, at the bar of the White Hart.' After a moment's pauses for reflection, he added something Conquest thought highly unlikely. He said, 'If I'm anything, Cliff, I'm a man of the people. I listen to my constituents *assiduously.*'

Conquest managed a wry laugh. 'I must try that with my students. I'd bankrupt the university in a week.'

'It's not just disapproval I'm the target of, you know? It's actual violence. I've also been threatened for having Royalist sympathies.'

'*Republicans?*'

'It seems I'm being targeted for having bright, positive things to say about everything.' A moiety of self-pity had crept back into his voice.

'Ah, yes, social media!' Conquest looked cryptic. He avoided it like poison and knew it was the most modish of the promiscuities by which politicians could expect to be tempted. 'I must tell you even the proper management of a university can attract something similar.'

'I was struck by what you were saying the other day about *disinterestedness*. I have it in mind that disinterestedness is like being a successful golfer who has nothing to say about anything, even hitting a ball. Such a person is the perfect embodiment of inoffensive excellence. I understand some of the threats made against me are pretty eye watering. It's been suggested the best thing for me to do would be take myself out of circulation for a while. Apparently, it's what MPs do; something of a badge of honour. The thing is,' he continued as he finally tucked in to his *crème brûlée,* 'our universities do a lot of international student recruitment. Tremendous initiative… Educating the world… Great British success story… Invaluable overseas earnings for the economy as a whole. You do it, don't you?

'Recruit overseas? Yes, certainly.'

'I'm thinking a fact-finding mission to our biggest markets might be what's called for. *Any good?*'

'Yes, I can see that might kill two birds with one stone.'

'Do something useful when I'm out of circulation for a while; gather insights about the things governmental agencies might do to help our universities, reflecting the importance of international recruitment and all that. Tell me, do you have an expert who could give me a steer?'

'Well, we have a Pro-Vice-Chancellor (International Outreach) called Professor Newell. He seems to do his job pretty thoroughly.'

'Anybody the other end? Someone with local knowledge, someone who knows the ropes out there?'

'Yes, I suppose so. We work with a recruitment agency. I'm afraid I don't have the details, but I could let you know.'

'Yes, good, *do*! Of course, I couldn't go without a proper delegation.'

'No, I can see that wouldn't be appropriate.'

'I wondered if you might care to be a member? It would, I think, be opportune. You see, there's a vision we're putting together intended to gain us some traction in Tory heartlands. I wanted to discuss it with you before taking it public. The element I'm leading on is modelled on the University of the Highlands and Islands.'

'Ah,' said Conquest, taking a sip of his wine. 'The University of the Highlands and Islands has campuses in a number of far flung locations, does it not?'

'Yes, in the far north. We want to do something similar in the south. To be specific, we want to create a university that links some of our largest and most notable National Parks. We propose to call it the University of the Wealds and Wolds.'

Conquest thought the name a whimsical joke. 'What about the Downs and Moors?'

'Don't roll off the tongue, does it? We've had the people at Scribbling Inc all over this for weeks now. They say the alliteration is attention grabbing; has to be the University of the Wealds and Wolds.'

'*Scribbling ink?*'

'Ha, ha! No, inc: *incorporated*! Public relations business: "*lobbying and communications services embedded in culture empowering the shape of tomorrow positively and creatively*".'

'Really?' In his many years of involvement in Higher Education, Conquest had come across many mission statements; he relished this, to his mind, grisly example.

'On the domestic front they're our official Strategic Thinking Partner. They have a Concept Team working on the proposal.' Lancing grew confidential. 'Of course, as you so rightly say, political disinterestedness is an absolute, but our National Parks are just waiting to be liberated from the fold of old-time Tory thinking. The University of the Wealds and Wolds will show the electorate in our National Parks that Labour can bring greater benefits than those produced by planting forests and nurturing wildlife.' He leaned forward. 'On the quiet, we're working on an endorsement from the Obamas. Do you know how many miles of dry stone wall there are in the Peak District?'

'No, I—'

'*26,000!* It's a national asset, but just imagine the upkeep! I'd like to see the Isle of Thanet given National Park status.'

'Isn't it rather too built-up to qualify as a National Park?'

'As things stand, yes! But there are marvellous walks on the Isle of Thanet. I'd like to introduce the rest of the country to them, on TV. In my opinion the whole national parks initiative needs modernising. English Heritage and the National Parks need to get to work on suburban sprawl; turn it into something people want to cherish.'

'That's a little *outré*, isn't it? How are they going to do that?'

'We co-opt the local authorities! We turn council tax on its head and give discounts to people who beautify their properties.'

'Discounts? *On council tax?*'

'Exactly: *an incentive*! And property owners that don't look after their properties, or cause eyesores, pay a surcharge on council tax. Front garden turned into a parking space: surcharge! Artificial stone cladding: surcharge! Cut down trees: surcharge! The same with business rates. Build ugly warehouse: surcharge! Petrol station signage: surcharge! That way lies the beautification of England. You understand the sentiment? A few other ideas like that will modernise the whole National Parks initiative.'

'Yes, I suppose—'

'It's an initiative we're going public with over the next few weeks. We'll be doing a whole series of Press briefings. We have a logo and catchphrase: "Put Your Boot Into The New National Parks": a play with irony. My University of the Wealds and Wolds is just one small part of a much bigger initiative. What do you think? Credible? Timely?'

'*Impressive!*' agreed Conquest, generously putting aside his suspicion that Lancing and his confederates were in danger of a collective brain seizure. 'But doesn't it all rather smack of having a policy?'

'Well, not a policy, I hope. I mean, nobody can argue with the greening of Britain, can they?'

'No, I suppose not.'

'It's a vision, not a policy. Modernising isn't usually policy driven; it mainly happens whether it's intended or not. Visions are bottom-up, policies top-down.' Lancing wanted to be sure there was no misunderstanding and he ducked his head self-deprecatingly. 'As an idea it needs bone and muscle, *of course*! Ownership will be key. I thought we could parse and scope out the pith, shake the tree – *intensification, connectivity* – while we're in the Far East, and then run it up the flagpole a few times to see who salutes... or blows a whistle.'

All in all, Conquest left the restaurant with a feeling of wellbeing. Inclusion in a delegation to the Far East appealed to him, but Marcus Lancing was a puzzle. Conquest had long held the ambition to enter the political fray on behalf of Labour. He judged he could bring a good many skills to the role, but he hadn't envisaged being an MP in the way Lancing was. This was a modern politician of a kind he hadn't met before. Those he had come across previously had been staid, inclined to the self-confident espousal of a conventional political creed, unremarkable. Lancing disavowed policies; policies were the product of what he had referred to as 'solidified group-think'. Nevertheless, he was brimming with enthusiasm for all manner of causes – what did he call then? "Visions, not policies" – which might have seemed a little tinpot considered individually but, taken as a whole, he had impressed Conquest with his sense of purpose, even mission. That he found inspiring, even uplifting!

NINE

Vice-Chancellor Conquest dumped his briefcase and topcoat as he arrived, and it wasn't long before his recently acquired PA, Erma Radisch – armed with the purposeful-looking slab of an appointments diary she always carried – followed him into the Vice-Chancellor's suite. One did not instantly warm to Ms Radisch; she radiated character with the pungency of thick bleach. She was a little past the prime of life but as taut as something strapped all over with rubber bands. Conquest thought her perfectly adequate as a PA, but others found her conscientious, attentive silences more than a little unnerving. She was an old hand at University London Central. When Conquest's previous PA had left to follow other career opportunities she had applied for the post, moving up from a departmental administrator's job in one of the newly streamlined academic departments. She regarded herself as a custodian of hallowed university traditions that still lingered in cobwebby corners but elsewhere were long discontinued. It was a self-appointed role she patrolled with expressions of ethereal martyrdom if she considered Conquest to be in danger of straying on matters of protocol. Other than that, she left at home every shred of her cultural baggage in domestic circumstances that were an unfathomable mystery, and of which Conquest wished to know nothing. *A perfectly serviceable placeholder*, he had decided on her appointment, having no idea what she was a stand-in for; having no idea what ideal he sought.

'The Director of Finance is here to see you,' she said with her usual chilling calm. 'He knows you haven't any appointments for the next hour.'

Tommy Ballantyne, the university's Director of Finance, was a chunky, big-boned man who fitted his M&S suits as if they'd been tailored for him. Their pristine condition spoke of a man who did little in them but smoke and read accounts. He was aware that Conquest had met Marcus Lancing for dinner the previous evening and he was interested to know how it had gone.

Reflecting on his experience, Conquest said, 'It was not unlike talking to an educated chimp.'

Ballantyne gave him a baleful look indulgent of the other's disparagement but intended to show he was not about to join in.

'No, quite right,' said Conquest, feeling reproved, 'It's not the time to mock the man. *I know*! And he *was* distracted, I suppose.'

The fact was that, for all his deficiencies, Lancing exuded the casual air of having influence in high places, something that encouraged Conquest's dissatisfaction with the scope of his own endeavours. Their association, brief though it was, had whetted his appetite for larger horizons.

'The point is, Tommy, as the representative of an upstart institution like University London Central you can only get so far. We're not really at the High Table, are we?'

'I thought everything was going rather well,' he said, a touch reproachfully.

'Well enough, I suppose,' agreed Conquest, although his voice lacked enthusiasm. 'I think Lancing sees me as a bit of a workhorse, not a racehorse; I'm short on the trappings of power.'

'I thought your new book was going to put that right. The gossips around the university are saying it's going to shake things up and make your name.'

Conquest did, indeed, nurse the secret hope that the book would aid his progress to greater things.

'Ah, yes! *A Plan For The New University: A Vision for Higher Education Fit For Today And Tomorrow.* Lancing wants copies for the members of his committee. He also wants me to go with him to the Far East on some sort of fact-finding mission about international student recruitment.'

Ballantyne laughed cruelly. 'Oh, you'll enjoy *that*!'

'The knowledge economy! It's a *"great British success story"*, apparently. *"The remarkable, still untapped, depth of the Chinese market."* I'm all for global link-ups and internationalism, but I didn't tell him our Professor Curtis thinks they're trying to steal intellectual property from his organic robotics research project. He's threatening to put up screens.'

'Actually,' said Ballantyne, 'it was international student recruitment I wanted to talk to you about.'

'What about it? Holding up well, isn't it?'

'Yes, but I've had a bit of time to work on a cost/benefit analysis. I think I've come across something odd.'

Conquest stiffened, knowing that when something in the books attracted Ballantyne's attention it foretold trouble. 'Judging by results, the International Office's doing a sound job, isn't it? Chinese end working remarkably well, in fact.' He looked at Ballantyne questioningly and, seeing his concern was not assuaged, he persisted. 'Our Pro-Vice-Chancellor (International Outreach) keeps a sharp eye on things, doesn't he? International recruitment has certainly been on the up since Professor Newell took it on. Seems like a well-run operation.'

'Yes, Newell gives the impression of having a finger on the pulse of the thing. Quite a professional, in fact. He's in the Far East much of the time... but there's this layover in Bangkok.'

'*Layover in Bangkok?* What's that?' It crossed Conquest's mind that it sounded like a sexual misdemeanour.

'He went out to the Far East for some recruitment fairs last month. Taiwan, Hong Kong, Mainland China. It seems he flew to Taiwan via Bangkok instead of flying direct. It's a matter of choice, I suppose, but I noticed he seems to have taken a two night layover in Bangkok.'

'So what: no connecting flight?'

'It isn't that. The same plane flies on to Taipei after a break of a couple of hours, but he chose not to take it. The thing is we have an invoice for Saturday night spent at a hotel at the airport and we have one for Monday night, by which time he'd arrived in Taipei. There's no invoice for Sunday. Judging from the records he disappeared for a day.'

'So you think what? He stayed somewhere else in Bangkok on Sunday at his own expense?'

'Well, that would keep the books straight, sort of, wouldn't it? And it was a weekend, so you could say what he was doing is none of our business, but I've had a look back and I think there's a bit of a pattern to this... And then I started to wonder what else is going on. I mean, he's flying out there to represent the university and all that.'

Conquest was sceptical. 'Professor Newell's not the sort for hanky-panky, surely? Even so...' He hesitated, his instinct telling him this was not something he should let go.

Ballantyne went on. 'Well, looking into it further it seems it could be something to do with our recruitment agency. It's based in Bangkok.' The detail required him to check a note he'd brought with him. '*Intercontinental Global Collegiate Colleagues United.* IGCCU.'

'Ah, yes, Marcus Lancing was asking about this.'

'But the thing is I don't really understand how our partnership works. It doesn't seem to recruit any students. Or if it does it channels them through our recruitment people in a way that disguises its participation. Then we seem to have quite a significant association with a recruitment publication.'

'*Publication?* What kind of publication?'

'It's called *Global Flight Educational*. It looks like one of those in-flight airline magazines. It's branded as an "*Education Around The World*" sort of thing.' Again he checked his notes. '"*International Travel As The Gateway To Your Ideal Educational Experience.*" It's innocuous enough but the small print says Professor Newell is the editor and seems to suggest it's published by us.'

Conquest was beginning to share Ballantyne's sense of disquiet. 'You mean we paid for it?'

'No, as far as I can see we didn't pay for it.'

Conquest mused for a while. 'Maybe it's part of our arrangement with our recruitment agency.' He stirred himself. 'Look, it's obvious, isn't it, Tommy, we should have Professor Newell in and do a little probing? Meanwhile, you should get somebody in Finance to have a thorough look back over the past few years and see what else turns up.'

Ballantyne shook his head. 'I'll do it myself, if you don't mind? Otherwise it'll get out.'

Conquest thought this wise. 'Fair enough. The thing is, Tommy, if Marcus Lancing wants me to go out to the Far East as a member of his student recruitment delegation I don't want any blowback from here, do I? My book extols the international race for excellence, although I must confess

I sometimes find myself thankful that China is a long way away. Do we have a face to go with this *Intercontinental Global Collegiate Colleagues United* thing?' he wondered. 'A contact there?'

'Yes, the Chief Operating Officer is a Dr P-h-u-t-t, pronounced *putt*.'

Conquest made a note of the name. 'But let's go steady and avoid Professor Newell thinking he's under investigation. We get a lot of income from international students and we can't afford to have him offended: he's much too important!'

TEN

Professor Malcolm Newell, the Pro-Vice-Chancellor (International Outreach), was teaching until one o'clock so Conquest arranged to meet him after lunch. Newell ambled into the Vice-Chancellor's suite, a somewhat otherworldly figure, a contemporary take on one of those jolly, benevolent characters from early Dickens: chubby, muted check suit, burgundy waistcoat and a paisley bowtie. Only the sharpness of his eye belied the general Pickwickian effect.

'It seems, Malcolm,' said Conquest weightily once they had exchanged pleasantries, 'that our international recruitment is being noticed in places that matter.'

'Yes, indeed!' Professor Newell peered agreeably at Conquest over his gold-rimmed half-glasses. 'Going splendidly.'

Conquest was studying the man, trying to detect shiftiness. Not a sign of it. He seemed cheerfully unabashed as though expecting Conquest to deliver further compliments. 'We were wondering...' He paused, somewhat disarmed by the blandishment of the professor's smile '...wondering how exactly we might anchor international recruitment more securely in the larger processes of student recruitment in general. It seems sometimes rather more detached than is strictly advisable, given the university's dependency on overseas students' income.'

Professor Newell nodded encouraging. 'Yes, yes, *very good*! I do understand where you're coming from.'

Conquest found himself lulled by such innocent enthusiasm. Professor Newell wasn't behaving like a man anxious to keep his tradecraft to himself, or whatever else he got up to in the Far East.

'Perhaps you might give us the benefit of your experience. I mean, it may seem obvious to you, but it's not written down anywhere what you do; how recruitment actually occurs.'

'Well, there *are* recruitment events. A friendly chat over a cup of coffee goes a long way.' Newell smiled winningly, sure that Conquest understood and approved.

In turn, Conquest, laughing awkwardly, looking to Ballantyne, hoping he might join in. 'That sounds terribly modest. I'm sure it must be more purposeful than that!'

Newell took a moment to think. 'Of course, long hours, a great deal of travel! Alumni are very important ambassadors, you know. They speak well of us and many hold important posts close to seats of power. Keeping contacts like that up to date is very important. I mean, they're influential and spread the word about studying here. *And* we expect them to be of increasing value over time.' He grew more confidential. 'We have several ex-students in South East Asia advising governments-in-exile. I try to make sure they know what His Majesty's Government's thinking is of their place in the larger scheme of things.'

Conquest wasn't sure he understood. He felt the faintest tremor of disquiet. 'Do you mean to say you're conducting diplomatic duties *on the side*?'

'Well, the Inside/Outside Foundation is kind enough to give me a regular heads-up.'

Heads-up! The term was sufficiently out of character to startle Conquest. 'Don't you think it ill-advised to be meddling in another country's politics. I mean… some of those regimes have long reaches!'

Newell chuckled. '*Ah, yes*, and many roads lead to Bangkok! But I only host cocktail parties for our alumni... and their friends.'

'You host...?'

'Well, yes! They're very jolly affairs and the recruitment agency pays for them. I just play *mein host*, and make introductions.'

Coming from Professor Newell's mouth it sounded perfectly innocuous, but Conquest hadn't heard of the Inside/Outside Foundation and didn't know what to make of the news that Newell was hosting cocktail parties and passing on governmental briefings. That seemed disconcertingly clandestine! Again he glanced at Ballantyne, who was stony-faced and, seemingly, lost for words.

'And the liaison out there? I understand a Dr Phutt runs our recruitment partner.' Here he referred to the note he had previously made. '*Intercontinental Global Collegiate Colleagues United.*'

'Indeed. A fine man, Dr Phutt. Went to Stamford and Yale. Ambassadorial duties and Honorary Chair in International Cultural Furtherance at Yokahama. Latterly, Chief Operating Officer at *Intercontinental Global Collegiate Colleagues United.* A fine organisation!'

Conquest took a moment to digest Dr Phutt's credentials and decided to call the meeting to a halt. He judged that further questions would alert Professor Newell to the nebulous air of concern that he and Ballantyne were trying to conceal. Furthermore, he was beginning to feel the need to gain perspective on what he had been told from other, credible sources. 'Food for thought, Malcolm,' he said jovially, 'We appreciate what you're doing out there.' And, as Newell reached the door, Conquest gave the impression of having a sudden, last thought. 'This Inside/Outside

Foundation... How come your briefing association came into being? I mean, who's your contact there?'

'Ah! Yes! Well, Professor Beardsworth is an acquaintance of mine from way back. We climbed Mount Everest together in '98.'

Conquest found this, along with practically everything Newell had revealed about his activities in the Far East, weirdly discordant with his appearance and behaviour. *Didn't he keep in his waistcoat pocket a supply of crystallized violet lozenges in a tortoiseshell snuffbox?* This latest revelation was dazzling. '*Really?* You climbed *Mount Everest?*'

'With oxygen, you know. So *really* that doesn't count, does it?'

Conquest saw Professor Newell out. When the door was closed he resorted to energetic pacing. '*Everest?*' he declared in the hushed tones of one who fears he might be overheard. 'I don't believe it!'

Ballantyne laughed ruefully. 'I'd better get back and take a closer look at what's been going on out there.'

Conquest nodded. 'I think that's right! What *is* going on?'

That was, indeed, the question of the moment! And, to seek further information Conquest's first instinct was to consult his most well informed political contact. When Ballantyne had gone he put in a call to Marcus Lancing via his parliamentary office.

'Hello, Professor Conquest!' It was Brendan Glendale, Lancing's Chief Parliamentary Researcher.

'Oh, hello, Brendan. Is Marcus there?'

'No, he's off somewhere. Can I help?' Brendan Glendale oozed condescension.

'I was wondering whether Marcus is familiar with an organisation called the Inside/Outside Foundation?'

'Oh, you mean the think tank nobody's ever heard of with connections to secret political associations?'

'I wouldn't know about that *would I, Brendan?*'

'I think they started out funding the Luminaries. Ever heard of them?'

'No, can't say I have.'

'Pressure group trying to undo the Wandsworth Road Forum's influence.'

'I'm sorry, this is all news to me.'

'Yes, well, I'm probably committing an indiscretion admitting to knowledge of the Inside/Outside Foundation. Marcus wouldn't approve; this office doesn't do opinions on the hoof, or policies for that matter. I'd steer clear if I were you, but if you must persist I suggest you try your in-house policy analysts.'

'*In-house policy analysts?*'

'Yes. I've been vetting your prospectus on-line; you have several in-house policy analysts. Most likely you'll find one with an ear to the ground in the right place.'

'You've been vetting *my prospectus?*'

'We're running a health check on your published works.'

'My university's prospectus counts as my *published work?*'

'*Of course!* You're responsible for its contents, aren't you? I'm glad to say it seems to be commendably neutral on the great issues of the day. I see you have a Pro-Vice-Chancellor Advancement (Form & Function).'

Conquest winced. This was a senior management role he had reluctantly added to his recent restructuring of the university's administration at the behest of senate, which regarded it as an institutional necessity, "given the complexity of contemporary exigencies".

'Yes,' he admitted, 'the exigencies of modern management...'

'In my opinion parliament needs to be more progressive on job titles. What is *advancement*? It sounds like something stolen from a car showroom. My title should be Marcus Lancing's Special Parliamentary Advisor, not his Chief Parliamentary Researcher. Much more appropriate! Sorry we aren't able to brief you on the other thing. It should be a game of two halves, but it isn't. Marcus did enjoy having dinner with you though; he'll be in touch.'

Brendan Glendale's abrupt termination of their conversation left Conquest irritable and disconcerted. There was, he thought, a definite air of the *Stasi* about him. Everything he said had the quality of a rebuke, including his refusal to be drawn on the Inside/Outside Foundation. Conquest did not care to be rebuffed in such an off-hand manner and he decided to discover what information there was about the Inside/Outside Foundation – 'a think tank nobody's ever heard of with connections to secret political associations' – in the public domain. Rather than blindly following the dictates of do-it-yourself, for which he had little enough time, he turned to what he thought of as a supremely disinterested gatherer of facts. He called in Erma Radisch.

'Erma, I want you to find out what you can about the Inside/Outside Foundation. There's a lot of questionable tommyrot in the air about it and I'm sure a little research with an empty mind would be very helpful.'

'Yes, Vice-Chancellor. The Inside/Outside Foundation.' She made a note of the task in the diary she always carried.

He looked at her, trying to make out what she was thinking. She seemed to be waiting for him to explain further. Either that or he had failed to make himself understood. 'It's a think tank, or some such, with links to the government, or at least to some wing of the Tory party... Some influential part of it. I don't know which, that's why I'm asking you if you could...' He realised he had fallen into an undignified ramble and he stopped dead. He threw out his arms in a gesture of mild despair. 'Bring me the bare bones... without any interpretation. *Yes*, it's interpretation I *don't want*! Oh yes, and there's a Professor Beardsworth who does something there. Find out what it is.'

Erma Radisch made a further note in her diary.

ELEVEN

Later in the day Conquest made it his business to run into Professor Fenchurch, the senior academic with the title Brendan Glendale had marvelled at: Pro-Vice-Chancellor Advancement (Form & Function). Having created the expeditious happenstance of meeting him, Conquest checked that the corridor was empty and they could not be overheard. 'Misha, I understand we have something called in-house policy analysts. I seem to think they're part of your quality assurance remit. Where are they to be found?'

Professor Fenchurch's looks and demeanour were uncannily like those of the Archbishop of Canterbury. He cast his eyes to the ground to think. 'Well, we have one multitasking – he's Polish – in the Centre For Silesian Studies and several—'

'*Silesian Studies?* Wasn't the Centre For Silesian Studies disbanded?'

'Quite so, Vice-Chancellor, but luckily it had a new lease of life just recently.'

'Really? And where else do we have in-house policy analysts?'

'We have several, one in the Department of Comparative Epistemology, three variously attached to the Social Sciences faculty, one in the Archaeology section of Anthropology.'

'Archaeology? *Really? What for?*'

'She advises on the archaeological finds chosen for in-depth interpretation. I believe her main methodological directive concerns the selection of finds originating at the greatest distance from the location of the dig; it's a promoting inclusivity issue; otherwise the optics don't look good.'

Conquest realised he was in danger of losing track of what he wanted to ask. 'What *exactly* is the remit of in-house policy analysts?'

'It varies, but in the main they analyses practices and turn them into policies, unless there aren't agreed practices, in which case they promote common practices. One of their current projects is to define consensual behaviour.'

'Oh yes? Really?'

'The consensus view, *pro tem*, is that for practical purposes 'consensual' should, in the case of interpersonal relationships in the workplace, be treated as synonymous with 'contractual'. We're also building a network of interlocutors in the parts of the university given to ideological strife such as the Department of Comparative Epistemology. Those attached to Professor Wilkinson's *Politics In Action* research project are advisors to the Students' Union on their policy options *vis-à-vis* the university. Oh, and they do the same for the Junior Lecturers' Advisory Council.'

'You mean they do that in addition to their academic work?'

'I think,' he said, with a faintly reproving air, 'they would argue, Vice-Chancellor, that that was a meaningless distinction.'

'I see. Doesn't the Junior Lecturers' Advisory Council advise the university's branch of the union on withholding practices?'

'Yes, I believe it does. And work-to-rule observances.'

Conquest sighed wearily. 'Couldn't it be said that in both cases the in-house policy analysts' efforts are detrimental to the best interests of the university?'

'Only if one takes a narrow view, Vice-Chancellor. More broadly our in-house policy analysts help to empower those in our community that have little or no say over the management of their lives. It gives the impression of plenitude that wise leaders always try to ensure filters down to these sorts of levels. It's actually of great assistance in the processes of selection for seniority.'

'Really? You mean they help us choose those capable of taking on academic leadership roles?'

'So I'm advised. It's all part of the *Build Better Faster Fairer* policy. Those most principled and coherent in their opposition to change are co-opted to change.'

'Isn't that rather perverse?'

'It's paradoxical, Vice-Chancellor, rather than perverse. Those thus identified generally prove to be safe pairs of hands.'

'I see,' said Conquest, forced to fall back on his stock noncommittal response.

'But *it works. And we are where we are!*' added Fenchurch brightly, strenuously. 'It's another version of the poacher/gamekeeper binary. To be frank, most importantly, I see policy analysts as *commissars* for free speech on campus.'

Commissars for free speech? For a moment Conquest baulked at the turn of phrase but then, like everything else Fenchurch had said, he let it slip away with measured equanimity. It was typical of the information that came his way in an unending flood. It might be consequential... or not. After all, if he felt moved to do something about the Junior Lecturers' Advisory Council he'd probably dial up Professor Fenchurch and get him to subject its deliberations to the oversight of a *pro tem* Advisory Councils' Scrutinising Panel.

TWELVE

Needless to say, Conquest was doubtful about the wisdom of consulting Professor Fenchurch's commissars for free speech about the Inside/Outside Foundation, but he was aware that since he had asked Erma Radisch to research that organisation she had been conscientiously peering into her computer screen. He was eager to hear what she had discovered and before she left for the day he called her in to receive an account of her findings.

'Ah, Erma, do take a seat.'

Seated, she hefted her diary into a horizontal position and opened it. 'The Inside/Outside Foundation is funded by international benefactors,' she said without preamble, looking at him meaningfully.

'Yes, good,' said Conquest, wondering if that was all.

'It provides financial aid and expertise to foster practical outcomes in support of good governance in all spheres of public life. It offers a wide range of short-course training opportunities and supplies trained dogs for police forces in third world countries. In the past few months they've sent dogs to Lebanon, Bolivia, Kenya and the Maldives. In the UK it advises the BBC on venture programming for young adults. They're also involved in the promotion of ethical hospitality and tourism in countries where—'

Conquest gestured for her to stop, her recitation striking him as increasingly unsatisfactory. 'Where did you find all this?'

'Oh, it's on the Charity Commission's website. It's their mission.'

He was unmoved. 'As mission statements go it's all rather nebulous, is it not? Nothing about passing on governmental briefings to third parties?'

She shrugged.

'And Professor Beardsworth?'

'Yes. Their website says he's the their Policy Director for Ethical Hospitality and Tourism. He's appeared on the BBC news as an expert on the Eurovision Song Contest.'

Conquest's exasperation was getting the better of him. 'What does the Eurovision Song Contest have to do with ethical hospitality and tourism?'

'There's a lot of glitter attached, it's very prestigious and generates a lot of *destination enthusiasm*. This is particularly valued by former Soviet Republics. The right to host it is awarded to the country that produces the winning song so they put considerable creative effort into their entries. The British government has a special interest in the contest because it's a vehicle for the increasingly pervasive use of English as a second language.' She snapped shut the diary with a finality that said the subject was fully dealt with and her work done.

Conquest was appropriately cordial. 'Well, thank you, Erma, that's most informative…'

But when she had gone he continued in sharper tones. '…but really it can't be right, *can it, Erma*? International benefactors, of whatever stripe, surely expect more for their money than trained police dogs and insights about the bloody Eurovision Song Contest?'

THIRTEEN

The following day Conquest reported to Tommy Ballantyne on his conversation with Professor Fenchurch in the spirit of a grievance.

'The whole idea of that post – bloody Pro-Vice-Chancellor Advancement (Form & Function) – was wished on me by senate when I re-jigged the senior management team. Why is it Form & Function? Isn't *form* supposed to follow *function*?' He gestured exasperatedly. 'Whichever, we seem to have ended up with a real dog's dinner... And, judging from what Fenchurch says, he's building a network of appraisal narks!'

Ballantyne didn't comment. He'd come with a mission, with much on his mind, and had been transfixed by the sight of a pigeon pecking at a cocktail sausage on the windowsill. He fixed Conquest with a confiding eye. 'Since yesterday,' he said meaningfully, 'I've looked a bit more thoroughly into the international recruitment business. Professor Newell seems to run a commendably tight ship. In fact, it's a model of economy, although there are what could be construed as anomalies in the accounts. We don't seem to be paying for some things. Or it could be there are invoices missing. Very odd! I don't understand the finances of the student recruitment publication. Somebody must have paid for the production costs, but it certainly wasn't us. It's not clear who owns it, although we seem to have received advertising income from it from other universities.'

'Really? That's rather clever.'

'And there are other credits in the accounts from other sources of income, but what they are I don't yet know!'

Conquest held up his hand as if to halt Ballantyne's avalanche of accounting issues. 'Fine, so you're telling me we're making money by selling international recruitment services to other universities?'

Ballantyne shrugged noncommittally. 'On the face of it, *yes*!'

'Extraordinary! Is it possible our recruitment agency, *Intercontinental Global Collegiate Colleagues United*, owns the magazine and our Professor Newell is selling advertising space for them?'

'That would fit the facts but I haven't found any debits to that organisation identified as such.'

Conquest mused for a few moments. 'I have to tell you it's making me feel uneasy, *very uneasy*! The murkiest aspect of this whole business is the involvement of the Inside/Outside Foundation and whether we risk reputational damage from being associated with it. Can it really be in cahoots with the government? According to Erma, the Charity Commission thinks it trains sniffer dogs and proselytizes for ethical hospitality and tourism. Brendan Glendale, Marcus Lancing's Chief Parliamentary Researcher, described it as *'a think tank nobody's ever heard of with connections to secret political associations'*, but he wouldn't comment further. He made it sound preposterous, but sinister! He also told me that we have a class of employees I wasn't aware of called in-house policy analysts. Apparently they owe their allegiance to Professor Fenchurch in his role as Pro-Vice-Chancellor Advancement (Form & Function). Glendale's advice was to get them together and see what they know about the Inside/Outside Foundation!'

Ballantyne knew all about Professor Fenchurch's in-house policy analysts. 'Ah yes, they're nothing sinister. They're part of the Pro-Vice-Chancellor's quality assurance remit.' But he didn't like the sound of getting them together. 'Not a good idea.' His counsel was to ask the Pro-Vice-Chancellor to identify which in-house policy analyst it would be most profitable to consult. On reflection, Conquest was persuaded and had Erma Radisch called Professor Fenchurch to his office.

'Now, Misha, your in-house policy analysts.'

Professor Fenchurch clasped his hands and looked deeply reverential. 'Yes, Vice-Chancellor.'

'Could they be considered knowledgeable about the political landscape, particularly about things like lobbying and the activities of private research institutes?'

Fenchurch nodded slowly, indicating he was selecting his words with care. 'Their outside contacts do tend to be extensive. Most have worked for one political party or another. They frequent the watering holes of the political class.' He lowered his voice in a model of discretion. 'Was there something in particular?'

'I've come across an organisation called the Inside/Outside Foundation. *A think tank nobody's ever heard of with connections to secret political associations!*'

Fenchurch repeated Conquest's words with creepy deliberation. '*A think tank nobody's ever heard of with connections to secret political associations!*' He frowned into his coffee as though searching for tea leaves to consult. 'On consideration, I would go for Ted,' he decided. 'Ted has been undercover for several years now. He's seen as a man of the Right, who's recently disavowed democratic institutions in favour of technocratic autarky and paternal populism. "Autocratic fragility" is his thing. He's excellent at securing very respectable research grants from think tanks and the public relations fraternity, which adds considerably to his credibility. He knows that world, *and* he's used to hanging his hat on strange pegs. He's advising the League for the Monetary Union of the Central Pacific on the adoption of a common currency. I understand he was actualising a proposal based on the cultural tradition of the cowry shell until he discovered the cowry with a capital C was already a crypto-currency.' He laughed harshly. 'Admittedly, a setback, but his project's supported by the World Bank's *New Initiatives In Monetary Management* scheme. *Very prestigious!* Yes, Ted is definitely a safe pair of hands and intelligent enough to know the lobbying world is a game of two halves.'

'Right,' said Conquest. 'This is Ted who?'

'Ted Bostik, currently attached to Economics. Funnily enough his son is studying Fine Art here.'

Really?' Conquest ushered Fenchurch towards the door. 'Thank you for your help, Misha. Greatly appreciated.'

He had felt tempted to threaten the class extinction of in-house policy analysts but he had forborne.

FOURTEEN

That Monday it was an early start for Dr Bostik, whose day generally started at about eleven o'clock. He was somewhat surprised to have been plucked out of obscurity and summoned to the Vice-Chancellor's suite to confer. Erma Radisch led him straight in.

Conquest greeted him warmly, although he would have preferred it if Bostik had been kept waiting in the outer office until Tommy Ballantyne had arrived. It meant there was an awkwardness, which he was required to fill with small talk.

'I hear your son is studying Fine Art here.'

'Yes, Toby: third year. Sitting his finals right now.'

'Rather surprising you should both be at the same university.'

'Yes, he was here first. It's convenient so I followed him here.'

'Where were you before?'

'University of East Midlothian.'

'I see. More of a commute, of course. And is Toby a painter?'

'No. Was, but more recently he's ventured into post-Duchampian objecthood.'

'*Ah!* And what does that entail exactly?'

'He's exhibiting a goldfish in a liquidizer.'

'*Liquidizer?*'

'Yes. Food preparation, glass. Goldfish liquidized

imminently... always imminent. I suppose it's the threat and drama of anticipation that's the aesthetic shock.'

'*Good heavens!* Whatever next?'

'Well,' decided Dr Bostik, 'it'll probably be some time before it makes the Fourth Plinth.'

'He'll have to upgrade to a goat in a cement mixer,' responded Conquest gamely.

They both laughed uneasily.

Conquest felt obliged to keep going. 'Didn't someone get sent to prison for drying a kitten in a microwave?'

Bostik looked politely ill-informed. 'I don't know.'

'I suppose that now people dropkick their cats and post it on social media it's rather difficult to achieve the aesthetic shock your son seeks.'

'Yes, but Toby's a vegan. That helps.'

'Ah!'

At that moment Tommy Ballantyne arrived, obviously having come in great haste. 'Sorry, sorry, sorry! Detained by inconsequentials.'

'Have you met Ted Bostik, Tommy?' Conquest gestured as though offering him Bostik on a stick.

'I expect so.' Ballantyne took in the man, his baffled expression suggesting he knew they'd met at some point but couldn't think where or when. He shook the other's hand rather formally. 'Hello, Ted, I'm the Director of Finance.'

'Ted's our in-house policy analyst currently attached to Economics,' continued Conquest, so bored by what he was expecting to hear he was already losing concentration. 'What kind of economics, Ted?'

'Social policy... sort of.' Bostik had an aversion to being pigeonholed.

'Well,' decided Conquest, 'we're on the trail of another rather nebulous thing – *institution, really* – called the Inside/

Outside Foundation. It seems it's a think tank nobody's ever heard of with connections to secret political associations. At least, that's what we've been told.'

Bostik's face lit up. 'Oh yes, that was Norman Bakehouse's brainchild. He linked up with Safi Phull to launch a number of research initiatives to help the Far Right deliver policies acceptable to Middle England. They were mostly concerned to promote value-for-money public services that didn't involve deficit spending.'

'That doesn't sound very Far Right,' objected Ballantyne, juggling a packet of cigarettes, knowing he couldn't light up.

'It depends on your political compass, I suppose,' said Bostik, smiling blandly. 'As a matter of fact, Far Right's a term that doesn't stand much analysing. I was considered Far Right when I espoused responsible parenthood. Why are you interested in the Inside/Outside Foundation?'

Conquest was circumspect. He had no idea who was, and wasn't, gossiping, but given the importance of international students' income to the university he wanted to keep deniable any thoughts of an investigation into their recruitment. 'It seems we might have been conveying governmental advice, provided via the Inside/Outside Foundation, to third parties.'

Bostik's face darkened. 'I see. *We?* Meaning *this university? Us?*' He looked pensive. 'Would these *third parties* be overseas by any chance?'

Conquest nodded.

Bostik was chary. 'They chop off heads in the Middle East for that kind of stuff.'

'Let's hope not!' said Conquest, laughing awkwardly.

'The fact is, things have moved on at the Inside/Outside Foundation. It's a work in progress and off the grid for very good reasons. It's another case of *follow the money.*'

'Meaning what? Meaning we need to be concerned about who's funding it? My understanding is that it's funded by international benefactors.'

Bostik made a back and forth movement of his head, a gesture suggestive of someone reproving naivety. 'Vague enough to cover anything! Look, there are vast agglomerations of residual hereditary rights and privileges in all manner of places other than the College of Arms. The mega private investment entities that have turned sport into big business are looking for new... *fields* – let's say – where things have been conducted, up to now, in a less than business-like way; where there are unexploited revenue streams and idle assets.'

Conquest thought this was the sort of talk that indulged the dubious and exploitative activities of private equity. 'There are economic opportunities everywhere, I suppose,' he said dryly.

'*There are!* For instance, plenty of vested interests wouldn't be averse to a more business-orientated Royalty. Someone like me, interested in technocratic autarky and paternal populism, can conceive of Royalty as an institution that both bypasses politics *and* is more business-friendly.'

Conquest winced. 'Sounds a bit retrogressive, doesn't it?'

'Do you realise what even a very small royalty on every portrait of a Royal Personage used by the state would amount to? *It's gigantic!*'

Conquest was beginning to feel like Everyman violated. 'Nonsense! Surely the image of a monarch belongs to the state for it to use in whatever way it sees fit?'

Bostik shrugged. 'One of the "international benefactors" – as you call them –negotiating to take over the Inside/Outside Foundation is a consortium of Royal Families and their backers. Let's say they're discussing how to leverage asset opportunities.'

Conquest's eyes were closed in an expression of distaste. 'If you don't mind me saying so,' he decided, 'that sounds like a consortium of ghastliness. Is it possible that some of these Royal... *interests*... could be governments in exile?'

'*Most certainly!* Look, you have to clear the cognitive smog. Big tech, private equity and Royalty working together might do *wonderful things*! I mean, charities are leveraging vast sums out of governments; NGOs are becoming the go-to experts on initial public offerings. The UN feeds more people than Nabisco and Unilever put together. *It's the new Capitalism!*'

'Only as theorised in the rarefied atmosphere of universities,' scoffed Ballantyne, suddenly livid.

'There's more debt than assets in the old economy,' said Bostik defensively. 'The old ways don't work anymore.'

Conquest, like Ballantyne, was more than a little exasperated. 'I don't see how any of this relates to the government's foreign policy in the Far East, or anywhere else for that matter.'

Bostik held up his hands as if to pacify his audience. 'I know it sounds odd, but one shouldn't make the mistake of thinking the term *government—*' here he jerked his index fingers in the air in a vivid mime of inverted commas – 'implies a monolithic entity; there are cracks and crevices everywhere...' Dissatisfied with the direction his thoughts were taking, he paused to gather them afresh. 'Believe me, there are many disgruntled persons of influence with hereditary links to rulers, here and elsewhere. Out of favour political dynasties with royal blood, *you know*? In circles that matter they've declared themselves the Fifth Estate. And potentially they can call on resources that make sovereign wealth funds look like peanuts! Resources begat influence; influence begets power and there is a whole raft of sympathisers in the Tory ranks. We may not know the whole story but you have to assume that the Inside/Outside Foundation is acting as a conduit between political interests here and in the Far East. It may be below the event horizon for the moment, but it has a public relations off-shoot that is definitely very active.'

After Bostik had gone, Conquest lapsed into a brown study. Eventually Ballantyne made a move to go, which brought him out of it. 'I didn't think we had people like that in the university,' he said gloomily. 'Do they teach students?'

'I don't expect so.'

'*Good!*' He responded with a shudder. 'I don't care for people like that, or their views. I'd almost rather have a Hegelian absolutist, any day. It's fruit of the poisoned tree!'

'Fruit of the poisoned tree is evidence illegally obtained—'

'*I know! I know perfectly well what fruit of the poisoned tree is! It's a term I'm fortuitously misapplying!* Damn it, everyone else does it, why shouldn't I?'

The force of Conquest's ill temper brought up Ballantyne short. It was most unlike him. There were wheels within wheels, he thought, and a wall of worry to be climbed.

For Conquest's part, what he had originally regarded as an anomaly in the university's finances was becoming a major political intrigue from which the university needed to be extricated. He wasn't sure how much of the information Dr Bostik had given him was to be trusted. His account of where the Foundation was heading seemed as deranged as everything else he had heard. After Ballantyne had gone back to his accounts, Conquest phoned Professor Fenchurch, Pro-Vice-Chancellor Advancement (Form & Function), to ask him how Bostik had earned his doctorate. Fenchurch replied that it was a PhD on *The Economics of Medieval Bavarian Street Theatre*. Had it been a financial disclosure made for the purpose of a bank loan Bostik's credit rating would have plummeted. Conquest was becoming ever firmer in his view that in-house policy analysts were an unnecessary staffing expense and should be done away with.

FIFTEEN

Teatime found Conquest in conference with Professor Woolworth, Pro-Vice-Chancellor Academic, a man steeped in a weak tincture of melancholy. Woolworth was tall and willowy, but in the manner of a willow beaten down by storms. He had come to discuss the agenda for the end-of-year meeting of Academic Board. Where academic matters were concerned, Academic Board was the most powerful legislative committee of the university. As a consequence Woolworth, its secretary, wielded considerable power and influence over the academic management of the university. Conquest chaired the Board and kept a very close eye on the agenda items brought to its meetings, but today his mind was on in-house policy advisors and the Inside/Outside Foundation.

Woolworth tapped the uppermost sheet of the papers he had brought with him. 'The Department of Tourism, Hospitality, Sports & Heritage wants Academic Board's approval to launch a new pathway of its modular postgraduate degree.'

'Called what?'

'Study Centre Studies.'

Conquest frowned, thinking something didn't seem right. 'Postgraduate Degree in Study Centre Studies? That sounds nonsense. Can't they call it something else?'

'Well, no. Study work experience in study centres is a central element of the course.'

Conquest groaned.

'Apparently study centres, and not just museums, libraries and local authority archives, have become important resources where all kinds of cultural activities can be studied. They're specialised collections where particular subjects are comprehensively presented, not just by books but also by documentation and artifacts of all kinds. Black Lives Matter Study Centres, Football Culture in Greater Manchester Study Centres, a Vegan Lifestyle Study Centre... *in Cardiff*, of all places. You see, they address contemporary issues that our museums are failing to capitalise on.'

'I rather thought,' said Conquest wearily, 'our museums were supposed to be the jumble rooms of an unfiltered past. *Clearly not!* Who's the reader vetting this new degree?'

Woolworth consulted his papers. 'Malcolm Newell.'

At mention of that name Conquest's demons were let loose. 'Ah, Professor Newell, our international recruitment expert! I should have known! Tell me, have you heard of a Professor Beardsworth?'

'I believe so. Wasn't he recently appointed in-house policy advisor to the Department of Tourism, Hospitality, Sports & Heritage?'

Conquest was shocked and appalled. '*He was? Here? In this university?*'

'Yes. I believe I've seen him on television discussing the Eurovision Song Contest.'

'Did you know he climbed Mount Everest with Professor Newell?'

'No, I didn't. I heard they sailed the Pacific coast of South America on a Balsawood raft. For several years Professor Beardsworth has, I believe, been teaching an *Eco-Frontiers of Tourism* module, based on their exploits.'

'Really? I find this quite extraordinary!'

'Yes, me too! I believe they were lost at sea for fifty-two days.'

No, Murray, what I find extraordinary, *Murray*, is that this man has somehow wormed his way into a salaried position at my university!'

'*Wormed* is a trifle harsh. I believe he's only *pro-rata*.'

'My understanding is that he's a strategist at the Inside/Outside Foundation.'

'*Inside/Outside Foundation?* Can't say I've ever heard of it.'

'No,' said Conquest bitterly, 'that's because it's a think tank nobody's ever heard of with connections to secret political associations. But, apparently, it's a power in the land!'

'I shall look it up.'

'Don't bother!' he snapped. 'You'll find nothing worth believing. And Professor Newell should inform the head of the Department of Tourism, Hospitality, Sports & Heritage that she is to find a different title for her new course. I'm not having a course called Study Centre Studies! That department makes us look ridiculous as it is!'

'If you don't mind me saying so, Vice-Chancellor, that's somewhat overstating the case. It is one of our growth points.'

'Ah, yes!' responded Conquest brusquely, disparagingly. 'Didn't I see a proposal from them for an BA in Cruise Management?'

'They have offered to take Fine Art under their wing.'

'Yes, because they see it as aspirational, eco, alternative and apolitical! I'm also concerned by how many in-house policy advisors we seem to employ. How do we fund their posts? I don't see them included in departments' staffing establishments.'

'Ah, this is Professor Fenchurch's innovation. The income and grants of all our research projects are top sliced to cover the notional cost of the support that the university provides them.'

'Are you telling me we've been using the top slicing of research grants to pay for in-house policy advisors? Is that standard practice?'

'The top slice does cover other kinds of expenses as well, like the notional cost of space, secretarial assistance and stationery! But, after all, arguably, it's research protocols where in-house policy advisors are most essential.'

'But *is it* argued? Who argues it? I haven't heard it argued, have you?'

'Well, no, but you understand where I'm coming from.'

Before Conquest could further vent his creeping sense of exasperation, Erma Radisch was at the door bearing a stack of government briefing papers newly arrived by courier.

SIXTEEN

Marcus Lancing was feeling somewhat aggrieved with Brendan Glendale, his Chief Parliamentary Researcher. 'Brendan, I understand I've been making noises about food standards, raising questions about why peeling onions no longer causes tears. Is that right?'

'Slightly disparaging way of putting it, but yes,' agreed Glendale reluctantly. 'One of our researchers did a deep dive on that.'

'And something about where has the cream gone from the tops of pints of milk?'

'Again, a graphic rather than the import. Annette has a research background in pre-organic foods. We thought we might test the water on food standards. It's a hot potato in social group AB, but our initiative ran out of juice, I think. I'll ask Annette to check if you're interested.'

'Well, no I can't say I am particularly interested in food standards. Isn't it casting the net rather wide? What's Annette working on now?'

'Pre-school meals. Or was it planning policy? I'd have to check my roster to see what she's doing. We're working on quite a few position papers at the moment.'

'They're not policy documents, are they?

'No, they're definitely pre-policy position papers. We have dressed up one or two as leaks from unattributable sources.' He thought for a moment before continuing. 'But driving footfall to your on-line presence requires material.

Soon you'll have one of the biggest ecosystems in Parliament. I'm taking on two new work experience students next week. They're going to be foregrounding defence.'

'Really? I don't want to be treading on the Shadow Defence Secretary's toes, do I? Frankly, I'm concerned my social media is developing a life of its own. Could it have been invaded by bad actors?'

'No, just the usual.'

'The usual? What's that?'

'You know, observations about policies—'

'*No, Brendan!* I thought we'd already established that I don't do policies, Brendan, not on the hoof. It's a house rule I don't have policies on my social media feeds, or anywhere else for that matter. And just to be clear, *Brendan*, your job title is Chief Parliamentary Researcher not Special Parliamentary Advisor.'

'Oh, I thought Special Parliamentary Advisor was nearer the mark. I do offer advice and it would sound a great deal more prestigious.'

'No, Brendan, *no*! And can you kindly find out why my wife has been invited to the V&A summer party and I *haven't*!'

SEVENTEEN

However demanding the business of the university, it was, at present, what went on under the innocuous heading of international recruitment that most concerned Professor Conquest. He had come to the conclusion that Dr Bostik was not a source he wished to trust on the matter of the Inside/Outside Foundation. Nor did he give much credence to what Erma Radisch had gleaned from the Charity Commission's website. A new twist in this murky business was the news that Professor Beardsworth was employed at his university as well as at the Inside/Outside Foundation. Not unconnected with that he found it suspicious that Professor Newell was the appointed academic reader for the Department of Tourism, Hospitality, Sports & Heritage's new Study Centres Studies course. Malcolm Newell's past association with Beardsworth suggested the possibility of all kinds of collusion, although about what, he had no idea. He could see no alternative to taking up the matter again with Professor Newell, despite not wanting to give him the impression his activities were causing concern. At least he could use his intervention in the naming of the Department of Tourism, Hospitality, Sports & Heritage's new course as a pretext to call him in to consult. Leading on from that he thought the best and only hope was to disguise any interrogation under the verbal equivalent of a lace hankie. Here, he decided, the chief motif would be perplexity.

'Malcolm, the title of this new postgraduate course for which you're the academic reader. It seems a rum business to me.'

'Ah, well, Vice-Chancellor, it's exactly the kind of postgraduate opportunity that appeals to students from the Far East. It'll generate a very healthy PhD intake in no time at all!'

'Well, good enough, I suppose, but I can't seem to get my head round why the department wants to call it Study Centre Studies. It reads like a conundrum. Can't you suggest they come up with something a bit clearer?'

Professor Newell beamed. 'Oh yes, I do see what you mean! I too yearn for clarity. Could we propose something together? A joint proposal would save me from causing offence. How about Postgraduate Studies in Study Centre Studies? By articulating the idea at its fullest it becomes clearer, don't you think?'

Conquest took Newell's suggestion to be an attempt at a joke until he saw the look of unblinking innocence. 'Well, no, I can't say I do. As I see it, that would rather compound the problem. I suppose I was thinking of something more radical. How about MA in Study Centre Management, open brackets, Theory and Practice, close brackets?'

'Oh well, that is *wonderfully* descriptive,' said Newell in a voice oozing admiration. 'I think that might even go down well with the department.'

'I don't like to be seen to be interfering in a department's affairs but, as the academic reader, it would be quite in order for you to suggest they replace what they have now, which is asinine.' Conquest judged it time to foreground perplexity. 'If I might change the subject, Malcolm, I've had a very interesting time hearing what people make of the Inside/Outside Foundation.' It was at this point that he had planned a baffled laugh. It came out like a pantomime sneeze. 'It seems to be a bit of a shape-shifter. Am I wrong to expect clarity? *Should I care?*'

'Not caring isn't an option, is it?' said Newell with shining sincerity. 'I suppose you've been hearing concerning things about it.'

'I have. And what I like least is the apparent secrecy. Surely our *alumni* don't bulk large enough in international diplomacy to justify government briefings from a think tank nobody's ever heard of with connections to secret political associations?'

'That does make it sound rather mysterious, doesn't it?'

'A great deal of what I've heard about it doesn't seem to fit with training police dogs or being a proponent of the Eurovision Song Contest. Then there's *Global Flight Educational*, a student recruitment magazine from which we receive advertising income. "*International Travel As The Gateway To Your Ideal Educational Experience!*" It seems you're the editor.'

'A modest contribution.'

'Far from it, I'm sure,' said Conquest with admirable restraint. 'And how often do you plan to publish?'

'Oh, once a year, I should think. It is by way of an experiment, you understand.'

'The thing is, I'm baffled by how the finances work. It appears *we* publish it.'

'Yes, I do like to think it sprinkles a modicum of prestige on us.'

'But the production costs seem to have got lost. At least, we haven't borne them! So I'm not clear who actually owns it, although I rather suppose we don't. I'm thinking that, all-in-all, our effort to recruit international students has developed a complexity and, perhaps a degree of sophistication, requiring some explanation.'

'Well, the Sino-UK Friendship League helped us out. They view our endeavours in a very favourable light and they thought we should do more to celebrate them. They wanted to profile our offering on the internet. We decided the magazine was a better starting point – a limbering up exercise, if you will.'

Conquest nodded mechanically, momentarily bewildered. 'But for the Chinese to help promote *our* universities for *their* students doesn't really make economic sense, does it?'

'Well, I don't know. I suppose the Chinese authorities don't take a narrow view of the matter. I believe we might be looking at a franchising opportunity. In our target markets a Postgraduate course in Study Centre Studies is the kind of subject it would be difficult for home institutions to validate. When it comes to private universities over there the more *outré* the better. We can hit the ground running or we're at the back of the queue.'

Yet again Conquest found Professor Newell's terminology oddly discordant with his demeanour. He was well aware that franchising was a common university practice but it was something he had limited experience of, and of which he largely disapproved. He had a sudden horror of a thought. 'We're not already franchising courses in the Far East, are we?'

'Vice-Chancellor, with respect I think the less—'

So much revealed, Conquest still bewildered, a host of questions yet to be asked, Erma Radisch's head appeared round the door.

'There's a man *here* from the RSPCA,' she said.
'RSPCA?'
'Yes, he's been here all day, investigating.'
'*Investigating?*'
'And now he's asking to see you.'

Conquest's brow furrowed. 'I'm in the middle of something.' He couldn't think what a representative of the RSPCA demanding to see him foretold. 'Can you get Professor Woolworth to see him? That would be more appropriate, surely?'

'He's being very particular. "*The Top Man*", he said. He seems to think it's a matter for the police.' She said this with sudden ghoulish pleasure.

At mention of the police Conquest decided it was politic to relent. 'All right, Erma, you'd better send him in.' He turned to Newell. 'I'm sorry, Malcolm, you can see I've got a bit of an emergency on. You and I need more time. Allow me to deal with this interruption and I'll get back to you.'

He ushered Newell out. Almost immediately a small, bluff-looking man dressed in an immaculate RSPCA uniform entered at speed. He had about him the unbending look of the religious fanatic. 'Sir,' he said without preamble, 'I come on an errand of mercy to keep you out of the papers and away from public opprobrium.'

'Thank you,' said Conquest lamely, at a loss to know what else to say.

'You have a student intending to mount a public display of a goldfish in a liquidizer.'

It was suddenly clear to Conquest why the RSPCA officer should be so determined to see him. When Bostik senior had spoken of Bostik junior's post-Duchampian work of art it hadn't occurred to him that the goldfish was, in any meaningful sense, a creature in peril. Now he saw the error of his ways. 'I can assure you, officer,' he said, feeling rather fatuous, 'that no goldfish will be liquidized on my watch.'

'It's not natural to keep a goldfish in a liquidizer, before the fact of liquidizing it as a *supposed* work of art. What has art come to, I ask myself.'

'The latter will not happen, I assure you.'

'With the greatest respect, we all know what young tearaways are capable of these days, don't we?'

'Yes, I do quite agree,' said Conquest, determined to be obliging. 'Cruelty to animals is not our thing. As far as niceties go,' he added solicitously, 'does a liquidizer have the right volumetric capacity to support a goldfish?'

'Sir, you have to think of the reputation of your university! It would be for the best if you issued a public apology… and reassure your stakeholders that this student has desisted.'

'Yes, I understand. You can leave it with me. I assure you it will be taken care of.'

Having reminded Conquest in the severest terms that if anything went amiss with the goldfish it would be a matter for the police, the RSPCA officer left. The issue of a public apology was much on Conquest's mind as he trod a circuit of his office. He knew public apologies were the staple diet of authority figures, but he was loath to offer one on the subject of harm to a goldfish on university property unless absolutely necessary. The laughingstock potential was only too obvious. Preparations should be made, he decided, but hopefully there would be no liquidized goldfish and hence no need for a public apology.

He had Erma Radisch call Sandra Torpington from Public Relations. While he was waiting for her to join him he Googled Marcel Duchamp to refresh his mind as to the cultural reference he was dealing with. As he read he began to feel as if he were floundering in a quagmire.

Sandra Torpington arrived with every sign that she had come in great haste. She brought with her a cloud of fluster as if she expected him to accuse Public Relations of some kind of unforgivable ineptitude. Before she could blurt out what was on her mind he held up his hands as if to placate a minor god.

'I've called you in to make you aware of a situation—'

'It's the goldfish thing, isn't it, Vice-Chancellor?' she said breathlessly.

He looked at her sternly. 'Yes, how did you know?'

'Oh, it's got out, I'm afraid.'

'Has it indeed? I suppose it's the kind of thing people take seriously so I'm not entirely—'

'Yes, terrible. Do you want Public Relations to issue an apology?'

He was disconcerted to discover that yet again she was ahead of him. 'Well, the time is not right. I mean, there's no necessity at the moment, but it would be prudent to be prepared. Perhaps if you were to draft something at which somebody in authority could take a look? Professor Woolworth, perhaps? That might well be in order. Could you see to that? Cover all bases, wring out some heartfelt sentiment? Do we have a public policy statement on the treatment of animals?'

'I'm not sure. We certainly have a Modern Slavery Statement.'

'A possible model,' he said darkly, 'with adaptation perhaps? Also important to remember we're dealing with an artist's right to self-expression.'

'Yes, disgusting, isn't it, Vice-Chancellor? There was a time when all student work belonged to the university. If that were the case now this thing would, long since, have been called in and destroyed.'

Conquest was well aware that public opprobrium for censoring a work of art was a possible outcome of the situation. 'Again, Sandra, not territory into which we wish to venture! Do your best, and get Professor Woolworth to advise you when you have a draft.'

With Sandra Torpington sent on her way, Conquest reluctantly turned to the question of the artwork itself. It was with some trepidation that he faced the prospect of putting the matter to Professor Archie Pomfret, the head of the Department of Fine Art, a man he considered a complete crackpot. Inexplicably, many in the university revered him. Conquest had them marked down as susceptible to the blandishments of an *idiot savant*. What was worse, since the affair of the student pole dancer he'd been harbouring a secret dread of the man. Nevertheless he immediately dispatched heralds to have him brought before him.

'Are you aware...?' Conquest began, hoping that by starting in mid-issue the matter could be dealt with swiftly. Pomfret was gazing at him with what he took to be a sly, sardonic expression but which, in actuality, was a window on a mind as inert as a flagon of argon. 'Er...' Conquest's perception was that Pomfret's chin was receding beneath his nose making the bottom half of his face seem acutely foreshortened as if he were lying on the floor with the crown of his head towards him. Disconcerted by the illusion, he felt unsure how to continue. 'Do you realise that one of your students—'

'*Ah!*' interrupted Pomftret. 'I know what you're going to say. You've received my note about the cancellation, and you're willing to step in and present this year's Horowitz Painting Prize. I think that would be most appreciated. Last year it was Clare Balding and she was a tremendous success.'

Conquest held up his hands to silence this flood of untruths. 'This is *not* about the Horowitz Painting Prize,' he pointed out. 'I have *not* seen your note, she was *not* Clare Balding and – *really* – she was *not* a tremendous success! She was embarrassingly ill-informed; she thought she was awarding an athletics prize!'

Pomfret looked momentarily crushed. 'Celebrities cannot be expected to remember—'

'Look, Archie, no more tommyrot. You know normally I don't expect to intervene in departmental matters.'

'Quite so, Vice-Chancellor.'

'*But* I have become aware of *a serious concern*. You have a student called Toby Bostik. It is not permissible to liquidize an animal on university property.'

'*An animal?*'

'A goldfish, if I'm not mistaken.'

'*Ah, I've heard about this!*' Pomfret began to shake with mirth. 'I'm sorry to say, Vice-Chancellor, you've fallen for the slice of carrot trick! Even those with acute powers of observation fall for it! You see, you take a thin slice out of the length of a carrot and conceal it in the palm of your hand.' He raised his hand to demonstrate. 'You plunge your hand into a goldfish bowl and when you withdraw it you wiggle the slice about between your fingers. Your audience has the impression you've snatched up a goldfish! Swallowing it before folks see through the illusion is the best part of the trick.'

'Archie,' said Conquest with a ferocious smile, 'are you *trying to tell me* that an RSPCA inspector cannot tell the difference between a goldfish and a slice of carrot?'

'Oh, I've seen some *very clever* people fooled by that trick.'

'I should not need to tell you this,' said Conquest with immense forbearance, drawing on the information freshly obtained from Wikipedea, 'but even I know that post-Duchampian objecthood eschews contrivance. Your carrot slice is a blatant contrivance, and if this boy used it in the liquidizer there would be every reason to mark him down for incoherent aesthetic adherence, surely?'

This caught Pomfret off guard. 'Well, if you put it like that, I suppose I have to agree. But I'm afraid I can't comment on Toby Bostik's exhibition. I've haven't yet seen it, and since it is currently being marked it can't have been seen by the general public.'

'Well, let's assume the RSPCA have correctly identified this situation, shall we? Obviously somebody – a fellow student perhaps – doesn't like what Bostik is up to and they've complained. The point is he has to desist. He can do what he likes outside the university and take the consequences, but we can't have him liquidizing a goldfish on university property. Is that understood? This matter needs to be resolved before the students' exhibitions are open to the public. Now, after lunch I want you to show me this thing. *And*,' he added, not without a touch of malice, 'I'm going to ask Professor Fenchurch to join me. As Pro-Vice-Chancellor Advancement (Form & Function), this is clearly an issue that speaks to his *form and function* remit.'

As Pomfret was leaving Conquest had one final thought. 'Archie, about the Horowitz Painting Prize. Marcus Lancing, the MP for Thanet Channel, is very interested in Higher Education. I think it would be most suitable if we invited him to present it. He might well have some warm and wise words for us, don't you think?'

EIGHTEEN

Professor Conquest, accompanied by Professor Fenchcurch, was on his way to inspect the goldfish in the liquidizer. Crossing Ramallah Green, they met Professor Spirakis, the head of the Department of Comparative Epistemology, who was also going in the direction of the Frank Brangwyn Building.

'Ah, Vice-Chancellor!' exclaimed Professor Spirakis in greeting, as their paths converged. He gestured towards the man accompanying him. 'I don't believe you've met Professor Linkage, have you?'

'Indeed not!' said Conquest, greatly surprised. He shook hands with Linkage.

'We've been discussing how to timetable Daniel's seminars on the politics of Involuntary Human Transactional Theory,' enthused Spirakis. 'He's also agreed to give the Fred Bartholomew Memorial Lecture at the end of term.'

'Well, excellent!' Conquest smiled warmly at Linkage. 'I suppose we should congratulate ourselves at having lured you out of retirement.' He took the man in and scarcely saw a retiree. He had a tousled head of hair and looked in remarkably good condition for someone in his sixties. Further, there was a kind of jauntiness about him that suggested a well-honed instinct for survival. 'But forgive me,' he said to Professor Spirakis, 'wasn't someone already slated to give the Fred Bartholomew Memorial Lecture?'

'Yes, a late cancellation. Professor Cannini wants to get away to Florence. We're lucky to have such a controversial replacement so close at hand!'

'Well, excellent, I'm sure.' Conquest turned to explain to Fenchurch. 'Professor Linkage has agreed to come back to add his voice to our academic disputations, *to our great good fortune*!'

Fenchurch held out his hand and Linkage shook it heartily. 'Excellent news, I'm sure,' said Fenchurch in his chilly manner.

'We're glad to have you on board, Professor Linkage,' continued Conquest, 'although I can't recall receiving a reply to my invitation.'

'Ah, I haven't got round to it yet, squire,' apologised Linkage. 'It was one of those institutional-looking things, and I thought coming in to confer with my friend Spirakis was more of a priority.'

'Yes, and *job done*!' exclaimed Spirakis 'Now we're on our way to have a peep at the fine art exhibitions.'

'Since I retired,' added Linkage with a broad grin, 'the student exhibitions are the only thing I've ever returned for... until now.'

Conquest's heart sank at the news that they were all heading in the same direction. He had the feeling that often accompanied the enforced politeness required of him as a vice-chancellor: one of losing control. 'We, too, are heading in that direction,' he said reluctantly. Despite wanting no witnesses to his inspection of the goldfish affront, he made a vague shepherding motion with his hands. The encounter, he feared, would turn into one of those anecdotes gleefully recounted over a round of drinks. His mood was not improved by the casual attitude Linkage had shown to his invitation. He didn't care to issue formal invitations that weren't responded to speedily and appropriately.

Professor Pomfret was waiting to greet them at the entrance to the Frank Brangwyn Building. To judge from the way his face fell as they approached he too was disconcerted by the size of the delegation heading his way. Nevertheless, he signalled welcomingly.

'Toby Bostik's exhibit is in the basement next to the bronze foundry. His notoriety is clearly spreading!'

'Professor Fenchurch and I,' announced Conquest for the benefit of all, 'are here following a report of an infringement of the university's protocols. We thought it best to examine it ourselves.'

'Sounds exciting!' said Linkage cheerfully. 'And we've come to see everything so I hope you won't mind if we tag along.'

Pomfret led the way down the stairs to the basement and into a high-ceilinged corridor of bare brickwork. When they reached a door midway along he stopped, possessed by a sudden sense of drama. On the door was a notice that read: *'Final Year Examinations In Progress. No Entry.'* They filed in through a heavy, canvas *portière*. Conquest moved with care, unsure of his surroundings. Facing him at the farthest end of the darkened room was a single plinth on which stood, almost at eyelevel, a large liquidizer. The glass jug of the liquidizer was illuminated from below by a concealed light source in the plinth. It was bathed in a greenish iridescence and swimming in the glow was the luminous orange of a goldfish. The effect was reminiscent of the hypnotic glitter that gives jewellery displays their allure; it was very much the room's centre of attention. Even so, Conquest's examination was cut short by something else that caught his eye. To his right there was a framed, poster-sized sign. It read:

Big Bottoms For Fat Blokes
A Proposal for a Crowd-funded YouTube Channel.
"Serving the Public Need for Big Botties."
Silent videos of Big Bottoms with Chaps playing Musical Accompaniment on the Piano.
All in the Best Possible Taste (Not Smutty).
"Normalising Fatness and Putting Fatness in its Place."
(Sponsorship sought from
British Airways American Express Premium Plus Card
to celebrate the Companion Voucher benefit, which could entitle you to a second seat for a companion when making a Reward Flight booking.)

Beside this was a small engraved plastic plaque. Bewitched, Conquest moved closer to read it. *'Big Bottoms For Fat Blokes.' 150cm x 120cm. Oil Paint on Board. This work of art is made to the highest environmentally-friendly specifications and is fully recyclable except for this plaque which is not yet recyclable.*

As Conquest read he was conscious of an abject Pomfret shuffling up beside him, as if to submit to the verbal blows he knew were about to fall.

At last, with strained patience, Conquest said, 'What *is this?*' He had almost forgotten the goldfish. 'Am I to presume this is *intended* to be pointlessly subversive and gratuitously offensive?'

At that moment a motley crowd came through the door laden with the accoutrements of internal examiners: coffee in paper cups, plastic deepfill sandwich wedges and manila folders containing the list of exam candidates. There was now quite a milling throng in the room. The chief internal examiner, a sprightly youth with sandy hair, over-large glasses and pale blue canvas shoes, smiled winningly and said, 'What's up?' Clearly at ease addressing his head of department in familiar terms, it didn't occur to him that one of those accompanying him was his Vice-Chancellor. Hastily, Professor Pomfret explained that Professor Conquest and his colleagues were taking a private tour of the student exhibitions before they opened. The illuminated liquidizer and its goldfish now had quite a congregation. The atmosphere was settling into something between learned and unctuous; only Linkage was openly amused, laughed quietly to himself as he examined the liquidizer display.

Conquest heard from the midst of the internal examiners a reverential voice: '*Nice! Sweet! Ding-dong!*'

The sprightly youth was a-fizz with enthusiasm. '*We,*' he confided to the Vice-Chancellor's party, 'are rather divided over this.'

Conquest's mind was on the basics. '*Is this,*' he asked in the sepulchral tones of one reading *The Wasteland,* 'the *entirety* of Bostik's submission?'

'Oh no,' the spry youth assured him, 'there's more work by him upstairs in one of the studios. This is a site-specific installation. A double-headed work like this sets its own criteria for appreciation. Some of us find his intention to be scurrilous is carried out with impeccable consistency.'

'It's on the border of mind-blowing,' enthused a companion of the sprightly youth. 'Even the site-specificity is consonant.'

Conquest was disbelieving. 'What, next to the foundry?'

'No, to the staff lavatories; they're on the other side.'

'And *we,*' said another of the chief examiner's colleagues, placing great emphasis on the "*we*", 'think it's puerile attention-seeking, without merit.'

A further colleague disagreed. '*We* see him in the tradition of great English eccentrics, like Lewis Carroll.'

'And John Lennon,' added another voice. 'The Chinese think it's terrific.'

'All styles served here,' observed Linkage in a lugubrious voice that could have been congratulatory or mocking.

'Given these differences of opinion,' wondered Conquest, ignoring Linkage's intervention, considering it to be his prerogative, and his alone, to enquire after the process of examination, 'how can you possibly mark Bostik?'

'We aggregate our marks and come to a consensus.'

It was with difficulty that Conquest refrained from demanding by what accommodations that aim could be achieved. He had to remind himself he was only there to adjudicate on a matter concerning animal welfare, not argue the toss with the people the university employed to manage the academic standard of their subject. His inspection, he could see, was turning into a circus, fulfilling his worst forebodings. Potentially, he told himself, he was in the debris field of a major incident; time to make a dignified exit before another round of wrangling over the cultural value of liquidizing a goldfish – or the threat of same – got under way. He had it in mind that when auction houses sold vintage electrical appliances they disabled them to insure themselves against the charge of selling them in a working, possibly dangerous, condition. Fixing Professor Pomfret with an icy stare, he pointed at Bostik's exercise in post-Duchampian objecthood.

'If this student wishes to keep this provocation on university property, cut off the plug,' he said, and made for the door, hopeful he was turning for home at Tattenham Corner.

Professor Fenchurch, muttering, 'Quite right, Vice-Chancellor, quite right!' gave the assembled lower orders the required disagreeable look and followed at speed. Professors

Spirakis and Linkage, having more student exhibitions to see, joined them in the corridor. Conquest was the first to speak.

'You understand, I had to put my foot down.'

'In my opinion,' responded Fenchurch, 'you would be quite within your rights to shut down the whole thing.'

'Hmm.' Conquest was not prepared to go any further than he already had. "There are several considerations here, Misha. We mustn't be seen to be too repressive.'

'Sometimes, Vice-Chancellor, repression is the new equality.'

At this point Linkage barged in with his own thoughts. 'It's voodoo art,' he said, 'conceived somewhat in the spirit of Billie's Three Rules of Personal Conduct. "One: don't be an asshole. Two: don't judge anyone. Three: have fun, bitch".' He laughed uproariously. 'It's a typical example of the reversion to the atavistic that modern society thinks smart. *Oh to be chic and primitive!*' He laughed again, indulging himself at the thought of the disjuncture. 'It's culture eating itself; plurality as a negation of values. Vegan milk chocolate thinking is artistic currency these days!' He made a gesture of facetious drollery, leaving it unclear of whose thinking he spoke. 'Or should we just call it adolescent bullshit?!'

The atmosphere from on high that greeted this sally was icy. Whoever was being derided – possibly everyone – it was certain no one was about to ask who. As the silence lengthened, sensing that Spirakis thought it politic to linger awhile, Linkage saluted his companions, oblivious to the chill in the air, and sauntered off to find more student displays, shaking his head, as if at human folly.

'I really didn't care for the tenor of that,' muttered Fenchurch as Linkage was lost to sight. 'It carried overtones.'

Conquest had his own reasons to be stung. He was used to a degree of deference from his staff and Linkage had shown little enough of that. Equally galling was the way he had gone off, apparently dismissing them from his thoughts as if they were of negligible consequence. *Unduly bumptious* was his judgment of the man.

'*Overtones?*' said Spirakis, put on the defensive by Fenchurch's disapproval.

'Need I be more *explicit?*' said Fenchurch frostily.

There was a communal pause for thought.

Professor Spirakis finally broke cover. 'Oh, yes, I see *milk chocolate*! Ha, ha!' He turned to Conquest. 'I'm sure he meant no disrespect to anybody. Let's not forget,' he continued in bantering tones, 'he's now neurodivergent.'

Fenchurch momentarily aped the goldfish, opened and closed his mouth in silent exasperation. 'Neuro... *Neurodivergent?*'

'Well, now he's no longer employed by the state he's permitted to think differently.' Showing commendable, but unwise, loyalty to his man, Professor Spirakis continued. 'What if he'd said *beige thinking*. Would that have been all right?'

Humourless though he was, it registered with Fenchurch that he was being made fun of. He appealed to Conquest. 'Milk chocolate is typical dog whistle wordage! Certain terms should not be employed in the cultural domain. I'm sure Professor Linkage has invaluable expertise, but that kind of language promotes the inference of unconscious... *selectivity*.' The author of *The Dismal Erotic* and *Language Hygienics & Hysterics, New Perspectives*, his most recent research papers, needed to say no more. He did. 'Even emeritus professors need to observe the tolerances.'

Conquest, who had taken his ease as a noncombatant

during this exchange, found himself – a pleasurable occurrence, this – in the role of peacemaker. 'That boy's arty provocations are enough to strain anyone's good nature,' he observed, 'but swallows and summers, and all that.'

Before moving on, Professor Fenchurch could not resist one final remark consonant with his remit of Pro-Vice-Chancellor Advancement (Form & Function): 'We can't have creeping censorship... but there has to be an unspoken consensus about certain ideas that are deemed excluded from civilised consideration. Moderating self-censorship must be our goal!'

As Conquest made his way back across Ramallah Green it struck him that Spirakis's defence of Linkage's comments about Toby Bostik's exhibition demonstrated a more than usual sense of loyalty. *Loose cannon* came to mind, although he couldn't quite decide to whom it was applicable. He tried to displace it with the sonorous name of his most recent lunch – *Barnsley chop* – but *loose cannon* wouldn't budge.

NINETEEN

Erma Radisch put an outside call through to Conquest's phone. Conquest picked up.

'Hello?'

'Can I speak to Professor Conquest please?'

'Speaking.'

'Oh, hello, it's Marcus Lancing's office here.'

Conquest recognised the voice of Brendan Glendale, Marcus Lancing's Chief Parliamentary Researcher. 'Brendan, is that *you*?'

'Yes, I suppose it is.'

So far their exchange had, as far as Conquest was concerned, lived up to Glendale's cryptic method of doing business. 'You have a message for me?'

'A couple, actually. Marcus would like the contact details of the overseas recruitment organisation you work with in the Far East. He's thinking about taking on a consultant for his mission.'

'Mission sounds rather grand.'

'*All-Party Parliamentary Group Enquiry into the Social, Financial and Educational Issues Consequent on International Recruitment in Higher Education*. It's—'

'Is *that* what he's calling it?'

'Rather a lot of MPs have signed up. We've registered it as an All-Party Parliamentary Group.'

'Goodness! It does sound *very* grand.' While he was speaking, Conquest had been scrabbling about in the loose papers on his desk to find the note he had made about Dr Phutt. He experienced a moment of doubt as he prepared to pass on the information... but nature abhors a vacuum.

'The recruitment agency we use is called *Intercontinental Global Collegiate Colleagues United*. The Chief Operating Officer is a Dr Phutt, spelt P H U T T, but pronounced "putt".' He gave Brendan the further contact details. In the backwash of conveying this information he found himself wondering by what academic route Dr Phutt had gained his doctorate.

'Thank you, Vice-Chancellor. Marcus has found some money sloshing around so he might invite him to London to check him out. I think we could manage perfectly well on our own, but he insists. Have you any objections?'

Conquest wished he could kibosh the whole thing but that would make him look absurd. 'No, no, good idea,' said he faintly.

'...Second thing. Marcus has been canvassed by a couple that makes current events-type documentaries. They've pitched a series to the BBC called *The Knowledge Factory* about the inner workings of a university. They've contacted him for advice. More to the point they'd really like his endorsement. He wants to talk to you about it; give him the benefit of an insider's point of view. Could you have lunch with him on Friday?'

TWENTY

Whatever else Marcus Lancing was, he wasn't an MP who liked, for lunch, to line up the empty vodka Martini glasses next to his place setting. Conquest had to while away twenty minutes at the table before he joined him. Even as Lancing sat down he drummed the table in an excess of nervous energy. Conquest thought he detected an evangelical glint in his eyes.

'I had a thought on my way here. I'm wondering whether, in pursuit of a general sense of their collective good, vice-chancellors should be seen to do a certain amount of charitable work... and that sort of thing.'

'Charitable work?' Conquest was puzzled. 'You mean as a contractual obligation?'

'Well, wouldn't it demonstrate that the bigwigs of Higher Education are a good thing?'

'But Marcus, doesn't that rather rest on their performance as vice-chancellors?'

'Well, I don't know. Being a VC entails a lot of privileges too, and over and above promoting the idea that they're a good thing for Higher Education, wouldn't it be great if we could drive it home by having them do public-spirited works supporting our wider communities? I mean, lawyers have a reputation for callous instrumentalism, don't they? And they off-set it by propagating the idea of *pro bono* work. Doesn't that offer us a model we can apply elsewhere, most particularly if there's a sense of reputational hesitancy?'

'I'm not quite sure I agree with the principle,' said Conquest frostily.

'On the quiet, I hear the BBC expects anyone on its payroll earning over half a million to be committed to activist goodness. They think of it as the base camp on the climb to national treasure.'

Conquest was unsure whether he should take seriously the impression Lancing was giving that his opinion of the role vice-chancellors played in the furtherance of Higher Education was low, insultingly so. He had a riposte at hand to put Lancing on the defensive. 'It rather sounds like you're developing a policy.'

'*No*, no, a talking point, not a policy!'

Conquest gave up. 'Then sorry, I don't understand what this is really about.'

Before Lancing could respond the waiter arrived with menus and wanted to take orders for drinks. Lancing ordered water, '*con gas*'.

'Well,' he continued, turning back to Conquest, 'the point is that we don't want an unsympathetic portrait painting, do we?"

'*Ah, now I see!* You're worrying about this documentary film series, *The Knowledge Factory.*'

'Spot on! This perfectly nice, intelligent couple has what it takes to do a good job but we don't want them overstating the negatives. Their angle is to look at the stresses and strains caused by the mass take-up of university education. They want me to give them my blessing on behalf of Labour but it would make us look frightfully vindictive if they were to dwell on universities' failings and shortcomings, so I need advice about what preconditions I should set. I was hoping you might give me chapter and verse on that sort of thing.'

Conquest was still struggling to get on Lancing's wavelength. 'They aren't likely to take kindly to having preconditions imposed on them, are they? Doesn't it seem contradictory to the whole idea of documentary film making?'

The waiter was back with a bottle of German spa water. He wanted to know if they were ready to order. Conquest ordered a glass of wine. Lancing asked for two more minutes and sent the waiter away. He swiped the air in an energetic gesture of dismissal. 'Student fees are a no-go area; student suicides, definitely not.' He sipped his water. 'As a title, would *The Ideas Factory* be more to the point? I mean, that's what we want universities to do: manufacture *ideas*!'

'I'm still—'

'Of course, the students must learn to think for themselves as well, then they can...' He stopped as if fearful Conquest might accuse him of developing a policy. Whatever the cause, he changed tack. 'My delegation to the Far East is turning out to be a winner. I've got more MPs wanting to join than there's likely to be places. The big-wigs have collectively sat up and taken note.'

'I thought the title impressive, ambitious.'

'Ah, yes, *All-Party Parliamentary Group Enquiry into the Social, Financial and Educational Issues Consequent on International Recruitment in Higher Education*. Rather catchy.'

'Sounds important.'

Lancing looked gleeful. 'It's been noticed. There have been ructions at Number 10 about up-staging the government's attempts at oversight. Look, all I wanted was to create an air of bustle around Higher Education. Now I've got MPs desperate to join my delegation. They're mostly Tories, but never mind, in large enough quantities there's prestige, even in Tories.' He leaned forward and lowered his voice conspiratorially. 'The point is, an insightful documentary in production at the same time would be the icing on the proverbial.'

'Well, my advice is to go for one of the Russell Group universities. I'm sure a university of that standing would provide the sort of outcome you're looking for.'

'Oh I don't know about that. I was thinking of something a bit more edgy.'

Conquest's pulse quickened with the creeping realisation that Lancing was about to propose his university as the setting for *The Knowledge Factory*. (Or was it *The Thinking Factory*? He couldn't remember which.)

'Actually, I was thinking your university might…'

'Flattering thought, Marcus,' responded Conquest, heading off the inevitable, 'but it would be two or three years too early at University London Central. We're in transition.' It was weak, but the best he could do in the moment.

'That's it: *In Transition*! What a splendid sub-title that would be!'

Conquest groaned audibly.

Lancing was troubled by the groan. 'Clifford, is there something you're not telling me?'

'Look, Marcus, there's a couple of complications I've been meaning to mention. Have you heard of the Inside/Outside Foundation?'

'I can't think I have.'

'No? I'm not surprised. Apparently, it's a think tank nobody's ever heard of with connections to secret political associations. I tried to take your advice about it some time ago but got Brendan instead. He was very cagey.'

'Cagey? In what way?'

'He said that since your office was opinion-free he couldn't offer me any information about it.'

There was a baffled silence as if Lancing had no idea what Conquest was talking about.

'Apparently somebody called Norman Bakehouse runs it, or used to.'

'Oh, well, I know *that* name. His wife's a partner at Scribbling Inc.'

'Isn't that the company advising you about the University of the Wealds and Wolds?'

'That's right: our Strategic Thinking Partner! Extremely progressive company; they use AI instead of focus groups.'

Conquest put his hand to his head and clutched a tuft of his hair. 'I'm feeling a little surrounded here, Marcus. Is it possible there's more than a passing connection between the two organisations? I don't want to say there's a health warning attached to the Inside/Outside Foundation but there are lots of conflicting ideas floating around about what it does. It seems we've been passing on governmental briefings to opposition parties in the Far East on its behalf. I've also discovered that a Professor Beardsworth who works for the Foundation has recently been appointed as an in-house policy advisor for Ethical Hospitality & Tourism at my university.'

'Really?'

'Yes, in the Department of Tourism, Hospitality, Sports & Heritage. I can't discount the possibility that the Foundation also has some sort of connection to Dr Phutt and *Intercontinental Global Collegiate Colleagues United,* his student recruitment organisation. Further, the Chinese government seems to be assisting my university in recruiting Chinese nationals as students. Lastly, I'm rather ashamed to say that we seem to be making a profit from other universities by selling international recruitment services.'

'I say, that's rather clever!'

'I do have my concerns, Marcus. Rather a lot of organisations! *I do have concerns!*'

'Is this any more than one of those off-shore fogs, Cliff? Look, Dr Phutt's on his way now; I'm collecting him from Heathrow this evening.'

Conquest groaned, inwardly this time, cast down into gloom and foreboding. 'Oh, so what... you decided to invite him, did you?'

'A face-to-face consultation, Cliff, is the way to go. He's as keen as mustard to come. Hasn't gone down well with my staff, particularly Brendan. He wants to keep everything in-house. *Ridiculous!* Leave Dr Phutt to me. I'll put my wife on to him. She's got a nose for things that aren't quite right. And stop worrying about the Inside/Outside Foundation. I'll have Mrs Bakehouse send someone to brief you about it. As Scribbling Inc's Forward Thinking Brand Ambassador I have considerable clout there.'

'*Their brand ambassador?*' Conquest's disquiet redoubled.

'*Forward thinking!* I help with campaign pitchpoints and the like.'

'Is that wise, Marcus? Don't you think it might undermine your reputation for disinterestedness?'

'Oh, I think, *I am interested*! Do you see? They've been supplying me with researchers to do work experience stints in my office: bright French and Politics graduates. It's no good having staff, you have to have *an ecosystem*! Brendan finds them enormously receptive when helping him with drafting position papers. Social media requires constant attention to keep eyeballs where we want them. Actually, Brendan is agitating for the job title of Special Parliamentary Advisor. He says your university is very progressive on job titles.'

'Yes, he's been vetting our prospectus.'

Lancing looked blank. 'Really? I'm rather afraid promotion to Special Parliamentary Advisor would go to his head. He has an impetuous streak.'

'So he wasn't vetting my university's prospectus on your behalf?'

'No, certainly *not*! Look, think tanks nobody's ever heard of with connections to secret political associations is Scribbling Inc's world, so I'm sure someone there'll be able to put your anxieties to rest about the Inside/Outside Foundation. At least now you can see why we need to be in the Far East.'

Conquest gave a wry laugh. 'I'm beginning to think we should avoid absolutely *any* involvement in the Far East!'

Lancing leant forward earnestly. 'One way or another, it's the future. And talking of the future, how about me putting you up as the first vice-chancellor of the University of the Wealds and Wolds? It would be a great step forward for us both. Think of the TV documentary as a job interview in public!'

Conquest laughed again, this time a little embarrassed. 'I'm sure you could do better than me!'

Lancing shook his head, complacently buttering a piece of bread. Suddenly Conquest had the uncanny feeling he was totally alone. His attention shifted to his surroundings where there was a sudden chill in the atmosphere. It was as if the whole room had twitched. Almost immediately the front of house manager was at their table.

'Excuse me, Mr Lancing, sir, we have to interrupt service. I'm afraid we've been instructed to evacuate. It seems a credible threat, of an unspecified terrorist nature, has been received. We're asking our guests to leave through the kitchen to the rear of the building.'

Without giving them time to question him, the front of house manager moved on to inform the next table.

'Damn it!' swore Lancing. 'This is the second time this week! This is why my delegation is such a success: we MPs sacrifice ourselves to be in the public eye and end up receiving too much of the wrong attention. Then we have to disappear for a while!' He tossed his freshly unfolded napkin onto the table and rose to his feet. Conquest followed suit.

The exodus of the clientele through the stainless steel curtilage of the chefs and their assistants was already underway, accompanied by a strange mixture of yelps of alarm and ribald laughter. Lancing, Conquest realised, was tending towards the yelps of alarm. For him the threat was personal and he was anxious to place a good linear distance between himself and any actual terrorist event.

'I tell you, Cliff, these terrorists are anxious to kill anyone they can claim has a hand in the till.'

'Don't you mean hand *on the tiller*?'

The correction momentarily eclipsed Lancing's urge to flee. 'No, no, *till* not *tiller*! It's a figure of speech, Cliff. These people believe they're fighting corrupt Western behaviour, but I assure you it's not unreasonable to suspect there's corruption everywhere. It's just that in some countries it's easier to get away with than in others.'

They emerged in a service yard that stretched behind several adjacent buildings. Lancing had entirely shelved the reasons for his meeting with Conquest and made off to find a taxi, still convinced, without discovering the nature of the terrorist threat, that he was the intended target.

Conquest remained, vexed that the opportunity to express fully his concerns had been cut short, particularly those about the Inside/Outside Foundation, and the possibility that there were dangerous political depths to his university's recruitment efforts in the Far East. Had Lancing really offered him the post of the first vice-chancellor of the University of the Wealds and Wolds? He hung about, brooding on their foreshortened meeting, curious to find out what kind of terrorist threat had interrupted their lunch. The more he thought about it, the more he was inclined to the idea that Lancing's mental processes hinted at a degree of derailment. Even so, he consoled himself with the thought that his dynamic ramblings were nothing more sinister than the vestiges of boyish exuberance. In mitigation, he credited him with the wisdom to temper this trait by surrounding himself with maturity and wise heads, not least his own. He saw himself as a counterbalance to Lancing's charming but erratic enthusiasms, a role that satisfyingly aggrandized his own importance as an advisor. And – a further consideration – he was beginning to wonder whether their relationship might not, in diplomatic parlance, be a game of two halves.

Finally, he walked round to the front of the restaurant where a couple of hyper-tense policemen were tidying up before moving off. Somebody had objections to a *Vacations In Israel* display in the window of a shop two doors down the street and bombarded the business with on-line threats until the proprietor had called 999.

TWENTY-ONE

Conquest arrived back at the university mid-afternoon. He was determined to make up for his interrupted meeting with Lancing by resuming his questioning of Professor Newell to pin down what was going on in the Far East. He had just settled behind his desk and was reaching for the telephone when Erma Radisch rapped on his door.

'There are three nuns here asking to see you. It's about the goldfish. Apparently, they read about it in the *Evening Standard* and came straight here.'

'The *Evening Standard?*'

'Goldfish,' she repeated.

'Don't tell me... Pomfret's failed to cut off the plug, and that boy Bostik's switched on the...!'

Erma Radisch looked at him with all her enigmatic self. 'According to the nuns, the newspaper says that instead of stopping him you suggested putting a goat in a cement mixer.'

'*Eh?* That's *ridiculous*! That's something I said in jest to his father... Damn it, *that man Bostik*! Erma, get Professor Woolworth here. I need his counsel right now!'

She returned to her workstation, where she had the nuns in a holding pattern. In short order Professor Murray Woolworth, Pro-Vice-Chancellor Academic Affairs, arrived, hovering in the doorway as if he was prepared to perform Twickenham-type blocking tactics should the nuns try to get in. He gestured wordlessly back towards the outer office where they had mercilessly canvassed his view about the university's treatment of animals.

'I know! Don't tell me!' Conquest gestured for him to enter and was uncharacteristically short with him. 'Sandra Torpington. You've been advising her on our goldfish liquidizing public apology, haven't you? How does it strike you?'

'Oh very apologetic,' nodded Woolwich. 'Heartfelt.'

'Unreserved?'

'Yes, unreserved.'

'Abject?'

Woolworth considered that for a moment. 'Yes, quite abject. An act of contrition.' He grew speculative. 'I did wonder whether there was something Sandra needed to apologise for personally.'

'How do you mean?'

'Her draft was one of the best apologies I've ever read. One doesn't like to pry but it adds substance to a certain rumour.'

'Rumour? What rumour?'

'Some sort of scandal brewing.' Woolworth couldn't keep a degree of melodrama out of his voice.

Conquest dismissed the idea with a grunt. '*Get a grip, Murray!* We don't have stationery cupboards anymore, they've gone the way of fax machines and duplicating paper!'

'Nevertheless, it's said something untoward is going on in Public Relations.'

'Any idea what category? *No, no!*' Impatiently Conquest tossed the topic aside. 'Forget it, there are more important things afoot. Those nuns running amuck in the outer office; could you speak to them on my behalf and see if you can find me a copy of today's *Evening Standard*?'

Woolworth was plaintive. 'They've already expressed themselves to me in no uncertain terms. What more can I say?'

'Say *we don't condone the liquidizing of goldfish*! And you can arrange for Sandra to release the public apology. It seems we have been outed. *No—*' he corrected himself – '*I* have been outed for compounding the original offence by having conceived of Bostik liquidizing a goat in a cement mixer. I shall deny actual intent, and attend to the denial myself.'

'And apologise?'

'Yes, yes,' he conceded irritably.

TWENTY-TWO

University Bigwig: The Picasso Of Provocation, was the headline on page 4 of the *Evening Standard*. Conquest held it out for Tommy Ballantyne, his Director of Finance, to see.

Ballantyne chortled as he took the newspaper 'Quite a splash!' He began to read out loud. '"*One-upmanship in art these days means a goat in a cement mixer on the fourth plinth, according to Professor Clifford Conquest, Vice-Chancellor of University London Central…*" Oh dear! "*His proposal for the plinth comes after forbidding final year student Toby Bostik to 'liquidize' a goldfish as a work of art. Mr Bostik claims censoring works of art is a product of a 'Third Reich' attitude to freedom of speech in the university, a result of the behind-the-scenes influence of the Inside/Outside Foundation.*" Tut-tut! "*It is widely believed that the goldfish was a slice of carrot and vegan Mr Bostik claims that no animals were harmed in the production of his art…*"'

'It's the Bostiks, father and son. They're trying to discredit me!'

Ballantyne laughed some more. 'You don't say! It says here it's *Higher Education Hypocrisy*! I wouldn't be surprised if this doesn't make the weekend papers.'

"Oh my God! Tommy, this is serious. I'm supposed to be the new face of vice-chancellordom, not a running joke! It'll undo all my good work in Westminster!'

'It's something of a five minute wonder, Cliff, although this reference to the Inside/Outside Foundation sounds a bit sinister.'

'I know. I did mention the bloody thing to Marcus Lancing before our lunch was interrupted by a bomb threat. He's putting me in touch with a public relations firm called Scribbling Inc. They have chapter and verse, apparently. Not that I'm sure it'll bring us any nearer knowing what Malcolm Newell is really up to in the Far East.'

'I did have a thought. I was wondering if Newell and Phutt are running an immigration racket.'

'*You must be joking!*' Conquest was momentarily horrified before regaining his sense of perspective. 'No, no, Newell's not shifty enough for that sort of thing!'

'I'm told there's a lot of it going on: the government has had a go at scolding universities for taking on overseas students whose only ambition is to bring their families here, circumventing the immigration rules.'

'That's never been seen as an issue at this university.'

'Maybe, but we know international students' fees are an incentive for universities to lower entry requirements. What if those doing the recruiting had other incentives on top?'

The idea gave Conquest serious pause for thought. '*Curious!*' he said at last. 'Malcolm Newell told me that the Study Centres Studies course he's academic assessor for is exactly the kind of postgraduate opportunity that appeals to overseas students. I thought he might have some idea about franchising it in the Far East but I can see it's possible it could be a vehicle for an immigration scam of some kind. Maybe the Inside/Outside Foundation's behind it!'

'More likely a private enterprise struck up between

Newell and Dr Phutt, not something a think tank would get involved in. It certainly would help if you can find out what does go on there.'

'What I keep being told is that it espouses a lot of topical causes of the kind the government prefers to policies. It might seem paradoxical but I'm beginning to think that the deep state stuff that odious man Bostik was going on about has a lot less impact than hospitality and tourism. I'm wondering if hospitality and tourism versus conviction politics is the new Two Cultures.'

Ballantyne gave a snort of laughter before reverting to his suspicions. 'I'm going to have a look into the possibility Newell's running an immigration racket.'

'Might be prudent, but go steady. And when you're going through the international recruitment finances see if there are any credits from the Sino-UK Friendship League. That's another angle I don't understand. Why would an organisation sponsored by the Chinese state be helping us to recruit Chinese students?'

At that moment Brendan Glendale, Marcus Lancing's Chief Parliamentary Researcher, interrupted their deliberations with a telephone call.

'I'm sorry about this mess, Brendan,' began Conquest before the other could speak. 'It's a bit of student nonsense that's got out of hand. What's in the *Evening Standard* is largely exaggeration.'

'Oh? Yes, I've already had a good laugh,' said Glendale guardedly.

'The Bostik boy is just a troublemaker. I can't believe I've allowed myself—'

'I don't know why you're apologising; nobody's formulated a response yet. Perhaps it's just a great human interest story and a credit to you!'

I doubt that,' muttered Conquest. 'Can I have a word with Marcus?'

'He's not here. He's gone to Heathrow to meet your Dr Phutt.'

'Of course,' he said grimly. 'I hope that goes well.'

'He's taking him off to his constituency tomorrow; he won't be in again until Monday.'

'Has he seen the Evening Standard?'

'Oh, I don't expect so. He tries to avoid newspapers. But don't worry, I'll point it out to him.'

'Thank you, Brendan, I'm sure you will.'

'He wanted me to tell you he's sending you his *The Knowledge Factory* filmmakers so you can give them a steer about what they're to avoid. I get the impression he was thinking your university should be the location for the series. Of course, that was before your goat in a cement mixer boob. Speaking personally, I've always thought it should be set in one of the newer universities, like yours. Actually, I think your present predicament offers an excellent opportunity to rehearse all the issues concerning freedom of self-expression so important to university life. You'll be a beacon of light in a naughty world and it'll be marvellous publicity for your book.'

'Thank you, Brendan. It's great to know I have your support. Rather more to the point, I await with bated breath to see what response the political nabobs formulate to this liquidizing story.'

'Yes, they'll all be heading to their constituencies for the weekend. Expect *vox pop* to have importuned them before their return! Goodbye, Professor Conquest.'

Conquest replaced the receiver with a sigh. 'That was Brendan Glendale from Marcus Lancing's office. He's already seen the goldfish thing.'

Ballantyne pulled a face that suggested he was unmoved. 'I see Marcus Lancing is proposing the Isle of Thanet as the next City of Culture.'

'Really? Where did you see that?'

'A very complimentary Daily Mail editorial. Seems Marcus Lancing is a coming man.'

'That's rather odd! He told me he wanted the Isle of Thanet designated a new national park! It can't be a city of culture *and* a national park at the same time, can it?'

Ballantyne shrugged. 'The Isle of Wight might have a better case. I hear ten percent is owned by the National Trust: enough for a national park in itself! They've got the Needles and Osborne House, haven't they?'

'Well, I don't believe either the Isle of Thanet or Wight is on the long list for the City of Culture, so there must be a misunderstanding!'

TWENTY-THREE

Marcus Lancing's wife, Vivien, was an asset: vivacious, sophisticated, well-connected. She was Chief Asymmetrical Risk Associate at the London office of an exclusive and expensive firm of American lawyers. Her skill was spotting the opportunities in the risks others despaired at. She saw her husband's politics as a board game comparatively low in risk and him, rather indulgently, as a study in lovable, muddle-headed charm.

It was a beautiful Saturday morning such as comes in mid June and, after considerable arm-twisting from him, she was driving his Audi in an easterly direction on the A2. In the car with them was Dr Phutt, esteemed recruitment czar of *Intercontinental Global Collegiate Colleagues United*. He had responded with commendable alacrity to the opportunity to advise Lancing on his parliamentary mission to the Far East. It had taken barely forty-eight hours from Lancing's telephone call outlining the rationale of the *All-Party Parliamentary Group Enquiry into the Social, Financial and Educational Issues Consequent on International Recruitment in Higher Education* to his arrival at Terminal Five, Heathrow. Now he was a guest of the Lancings, to Vivien's considerable inconvenience, on his way with them to their weekend home in Lancing's constituency, Thanet Channel.

Lancing was seated in the rear of the car surrounded by briefing papers. Since leaving London he had been preoccupied by a constant stream of calls from Westminster, and Vivien had been entertaining Dr Phut with improbable but true stories of her childhood in Menton.

'We all like young flesh, do we not?' Dr Phutt was saying to her. He was a small, wiry man, smooth and dapper to the point of being a cartoon. He had listened to her in appreciative silence for a good while now and considered it was his turn to test her metal. 'In Singapore my father started work as a counting house wallah. It's interesting how the language of such things has changed. Now I'm a Chief Operating Officer. You have Capitalism, we celebrate competition with flags and bouquets of flowers, and eliminate competitors with goodwill. You never eat sheep, or mutton; you eat lamb. *Is it not so?* You have lamb, we have the suckling pig. One can find very good lamb in Dagenham. Have you ever eaten in Dagenham?'

Vivien glanced at him, a slight frown crossing her delicate features. 'No.'

'The restaurant scene in Dagenham is very progressive. I especially like those girls with pale complexions and lovely pink cheeks. I think you call them *English roses*, do you not? Surprisingly obedient, once they've learnt the ropes. Preferable to the trollops we used to get from Laos. In the days of the white slave trade we had splendid girls from Swiss finishing schools. The consulate in Lucerne was most accommodating. Now we have the vulgar trade in economic migrants and stateless persons going the other way. As you Brits say—' he gave what seemed like a regretful sigh – 'the wheels have come off the bloody bus!'

Vivien studied him for a long moment with a slight smile on her lips. 'I do believe you're teasing me, Dr Phutt!' she said, her eyes back on the road. 'You're playing on what you assume are my presumptions about your cultural norms, are you not?'

Dr Phutt laughed and gave a small, regretful bow. 'I'm sorry, dear lady, my journey has been long and it was but jest.'

'No, a little more than that, I think. You were testing me, you naughty thing!'

'You are, indeed, a fascinating creature and I was carried away. Will you forgive me?'

'Yes, well, that sort of thing is very wicked, you know, but it's the kind of thing I've grown accustomed to since Marcus became an MP. I was at a cocktail party when an indigenous Canadian announced she was a lumberjack. Her aim, I suspect, was somewhat similar to yours. That was just before Marcus decided having views was perilous.'

'*What* was perilous?' demanded Lancing as he belatedly tuned in to what they were saying.

'Oh, nothing, darling. Dr Phutt was making me his exotic other. I think he's something of a tease, aren't you?'

Dr Phutt demurred gracefully. 'I must confess I have not been to Dagenham, but I was told there was a very good Polish restaurant in the High Street.'

When they arrived at their constituency home – a low, many-gabled house built in a rather fainthearted response to the ideals of the Arts & Crafts movement – Lancing climbed out of the car and took a deep breath. His loyalty to Thanet Channel was such that he liked to think its air was purer, more zestful than ordinary air. He thought of it as *Parfum Brises de Mer*. The house was almost at the highpoint of the constituency; one of the few properties insurable against flood damage. As he approached the front door he saw an envelope was tucked in between the door and the doorjamb. He opened the envelope and unfolded the contents: a sheet of lined paper. This is what he read.

> *To Marcus Lancing MP.*
> *We are as a human race living perilous time. We are moving from one disaster to another. Do you worry about the future not knowing the way out? We have a god Jehovah God who will eradicate all of mankind problems. Just a little longer, and the wicked will be no more. Politics and those who bring death, suffering, crying and pain will be no more. You will be no more. You, the ungodly who have offended against His Word will burn in the flames of righteousness. You will look to find the wicked and they will be no more.*
> *Sincerely, Enoch Death's Head Moth.*

Lancing looked about him as if fearful the perpetrator of this threatening missive might be close at hand. The shrubs hemming in the drive had taken on a menacing aspect, but the sky above was still a bland, baby blue. He didn't know what to think. Materially, the letter had something of a suicide note about it, scrawled in a feverish hand on a scrap of paper. Godlessness, it seemed, was being added to the beliefs that the great British public held against him. Meanwhile, Vivien was looking at him quizzically.

'What is it, darling?'

Wordlessly he held out the note to her. She read it, exclaiming mildly at the more apocalyptic passages. 'This is that mad old woman, Mrs Potterton, who lives down the road and votes bloody Tory,' she said.

'Enoch's a man's name,' he objected. 'You can't be sure it's not the vicar at All Saints.'

'*What?* Calling himself Death's Head Moth? Why on Earth would you think *that*?'

'He wants Tony Blair sent to The Hague. I'm tainted by association, apparently'

'*No! Definitely Potterton!*'

'How can you know that?' he said mournfully.

'Last winter I went to the supermarket for her. Her shopping list looked exactly like this. It's a lot of nonsense; she goes to one of those extremist churches in Ramsgate. She's hoping to arrange your salvation, that's all.' She moved closer, fixing him with her clarifying gaze. 'Take no notice; don't let it get under your skin! It's zero percent stuff.' She made a ball of the letter, tossed it into the bushes and returned to Dr Phutt to show him into the house.

Once he was alone Lancing retrieved the letter and stowed it in the inside pocket of his jacket. He was reluctant to accept Vivien's certainty, although he didn't dismiss it as wholly cavalier since he respected her ability as an assessor of risk. As a rule she made light of the threats he received, treating them as evidence of nothing more than the usual, unfocused, widespread hooliganism. Even so, he deemed the letter unsettling enough to make him think he should report it to the authorities when he got back to London. It also affirmed his plans to be out of the country for a while, although he didn't care much for this Dr Phutt who was flirting so outrageously with his wife. However, on the whole it was something he was inured to; Vivien attracted men like celebrities mobbing a good cause. It didn't turn her head since she had long taken it as her right. As for him, he would get rid of Phutt unless he provided good contacts.

Later, over cocktails, Dr Phutt returned to his scallywag mode, coaxed by Vivien in her husband's absence. She was beginning to wonder whether there might be something of the human booby-trap about him. Suitably primed, he was giving her his view of the world as seen from Bangkok, and of what he knew about the Inside/Outside Foundation.

'Those who wish you ill, I think, have more distant horizons when they paint the landscape of the future,' he mused, taking a first sip of his second Negroni. 'Ownership of the political heights for four or five years is insufficient to turn this boxing match on its head. Ducks crossing the road will tell you as much. Confucian economic policies out-match what can be done in a democracy. Your political class is a mediocracy. Democracies allow idiots to be in charge because no one with enough intelligence to have real earning power would dream of being a politician.

'Too much about Britain is shabby and dingy; too many rank northern towns populated by ingrates. Smart technocratic elites are the only answer to the ills of overpopulation. That's what the Inside/Outside Foundation espouses, and its influencers believe foregrounding policies that will cater for everyone is the way forward. In particular, they appreciate the significance of real grassroots initiatives like tourism and hospitality for all. It's the tangible something-for-everyone that will supersede the democratic tokenism of the vote. Too often here tourism and hospitality means pizza and fully-loaded chips. For the undiscerning sons and daughters of Christendom there will always be reservations on the shores of the Persian Gulf with free minibars, 24-hour buffets and karaoke hen nights. Tourism and hospitality is a huge industry and a huge number of Chinese people want to visit Britain. There needs to be an enormous expansion in catering staff and receptionists for new hotels with better facilities, suitable for the elite Chinese tourist, built close to cathedral closes, at World Heritage Sites and the like. Why is the National Trust not a hotel chain? Britain has opportunities but they're not properly directed. Universities are part of the answer and part of the problem too! There's far too much *laissez-faire* university education going on instead of Brits being trained to get behind tourism and hospitality. The Inside/Outside Foundation is gung-ho to set new standards and offers new insights such as these to international opinion formers and influencers, especially the new class of American venture capitalists.'

By eight thirty the Negronis and jetlag were further unravelling his pronouncements, his discretion and his brain.

'It seems the strategy of the long-heads at the Sino-UK Friendship League is the promotion of vulgarity and self-disgust. They see it as a race to the bottom that will have ever-broader cultural consequences. In the end it will undermine the West's belief in the necessity of democracy as the political underpinning of a modern society. People in democratic countries have been bullied into thinking they have free-floating agency, but their liberal individualism condemns them to a Friday night existence without principles, values or moral compass. Plentiful drugs certainly help. At some point the forces of benign autocracy and recycling autarchy will step in since such sheepish people will not fight for anything. The power company that keeps the lights on in the crumbling edifice that is the Enlightenment Project is run by Russians. The political class of Europe is indistinguishable from the contestants of the Eurovision Song Contest; the same voices, the same populism, the same vote-seeking. You gave the world the two-piece suit, but now it is an empty signifier. Today, for the rest of the world, it is the Eurovision Song Contest that expresses the true spirit of Europe, does it not? Your enemies, too, would love to cross-dress in pink leotards by Gucci but their calling is higher! I tell you Westerners these truths, but nobody listens. One day I will be boiled brains in a bucket and no one will care. The heel of the American redneck is crushing the delicate throat of the Bloomsbury muse while the Chinese mandarin seduces with ever-cheaper, multi-function personal organisers. England needs more than gardening gurus, and the more I say this the more my future is threatened.'

Vivien couldn't decide whether Dr Phutt was a jet-lagged, brain-damaged conspiracy theorist or a reluctant informant on visionary forces intent on destroying the West. Either way, in counter distinction to the anonymous letter her husband had found lodged in their doorjamb, she thought his threat rating on the occupational hazard risk scale was uncomfortably high. 'Existential' was the adjective that came to mind.

TWENTY-FOUR

While Vivien was engaging Dr Phutt's attention, Lancing was permitted the luxury of taking himself off for an hour or so to call in at the White Hart and have his weekly pint with the Labour regulars. He thought of it as 'grassroots liaison and constituency briefing'. The usual crowd was there and, beer in hand, he quickly found himself wallowing in the minutia of local happenings, He, in turn, was happy to give a careful, sanitised account of some of the more significant political developments at Westminster. His mood was perhaps a little more sombre than usual because of the garbled Old Testament curse tucked inside his wallet. Although, like the graffiti sacking of his constituency office, it was indicative of hostile forces at work in his constituency, he was not tempted to bring the letter out and see whether Bill Ashford or Tom Tudor thought it might be the work of the vicar of All Saints. Curiously enough, as he was brooding on the letter, somebody mentioned Mrs Potterton, Vivien's suspect in the matter, shaking him out of his reverie.

'What was that about Mrs Potterton?' he enquired of the speaker, Mr Foreshore, the geography teacher at the local comprehensive. 'I didn't catch what you said.'

'Oh, I've heard about *this*!' said Tom Tudor. 'It's her cats!'

'Yes!' Foreshore laughed into his pint. 'Somebody's been shaving them!'

Lancing was bemused. 'Shaved her cats?'

'Yes, some bloody troublemaker, thinks he's funny, has been catching Mrs Potterton's cats and shaving them.'

'What, all over?"

'No. like poodles, in patches.'

'Perhaps she's done it herself,' said Lancing grimly.

'To keep her kittens from becoming mittens,' said Bill Ashford.

'Kittens into mittens! Cats into hats!' declaimed Foreshore, raising his pint ceilingwards.

'Cats into hats! Kittens into mittens!' crooned Tom Tudor in simpering tones. 'Puss-in-Boots into thermal suits and Pussykins into fur napkins!'

There was raucous hilarity mixed with meowing.

Lancing was still brooding on the letter and the possibility Mrs Potterton had written it. 'How many cats does the bloody woman have?' he wondered.

'Umpteen of them, poor, semi-naked little pussies.'

'Seriously,' he ruminated, 'multiple cat ownership shouldn't be allowed unless licenced. And that sort of thing is a stain on the constituency! Damned if I do, damned if I don't is all very well, but I try to see all sides of everything, so why…. *Why* am I constantly being pigeonholed? Royalist, atheist, Blairite and now you lot cat carousing!'

His drinking companions laughter was uproarious. They were thinking how great it was that their parliamentary representative was able to let his hair down in their company with some zany pub chatter. Little did they realise that hostile forces were eavesdropping from the shadows.

TWENTY-FIVE

First thing Monday morning and the Chief Whip was gravely reading the anonymous letter Marcus Lancing had found at his constituency home. 'Your troubles are multiplying,' he said in tones that suggested it was Lancing who doing the compounding. 'Who is this Enoch character?'

'I did think it might be the vicar of one of my constituency's churches, All Saints.'

The Chief Whip tut-tutted. 'Once you offend your religious leaders you're in danger of alienating your electorate.'

'Vivien says it's a local pensioner.'

'Your wife says that?'

'Yes. She doesn't take the letter seriously.'

'No? One shouldn't be too sanguine. *Royalist! Blairite! And now Godlessness!* That's *not* a good mix!'

'I don't hold *any* convictions beyond the benign adherence of a sceptic,' protested Lancing. 'I'm accused of a belief I've been careful not to declare, one way or the other.'

'You perhaps made an unguarded statement. Could it have been on social media at all?' The Chief Whip fixed him with a severe stare.

'I did say that whether or not God was a fictive being, he was an active force at work in the world.'

'Oh dear, "fictive" has the stamp of intellectualism!'

'I was trying to avoid being definitive!'

'And this was posted on-line?'

'No, I said it at a meeting of the Thanet Tomato Growers' Association. It was an aside, really.'

'An unguarded aside, I should think.'

'Yes. I was giving the Veuve Clicquot Award for Exemplary Dedication.'

'To what?'

'Furtherance of the Urban Greening Agenda.'

'Always good to be associated with that sort of thing. But you went off-script?'

'Yes, I suppose I did. There was a lot of enthusiasm in the room. And reverence for unstinting public service.'

'Ummm. I suppose it might have been reported somewhere. In one of the local papers perhaps?' The Chief Whip wafted the letter thoughtfully. 'I'll get this to the intelligence people for analysis. But for staff shortages they'd send a team and ferret out this person. We could be talking about hate crime. Meanwhile, bear in mind your name's coming up in electronic chatter. It might be as well to check underneath your car first thing in the morning.'

'Check? For *what*?'

'Anything that doesn't look like bog-standard car engineering. Better still, I could offer you a distress top-up from the Parliamentary Contingency Fund to assist your plans to disappear for a while. How are they going?'

'Good. I've registered an All-Party Parliamentary Group: *An Enquiry into the Social, Financial and Educational Issues Pertaining to International Recruitment in Higher Education*. I'm taking a delegation to the Far East.'

'Ah, yes, I've had a note about that. As a reason for being out of the country it shows ingenuity, but I hope it isn't a mistake to have attracted so many Conservatives. You're becoming quite a prominent member of his Majesty's Opposition and if any of them came to harm while you're in the Far East it would most definitely look like political manoeuvring. How are the arrangements going?'

'I've brought over a counter-party based in Bangkok to help with the groundwork: *Intercontinental Global Collegiate Colleagues United.* The COO is a Dr Phutt.'

'Ah, indeed, *Dr Phutt*!'

'Yes, he's advising about what governmental organisations we might meet out there.'

'I have to warn you that Chinese interests are looking for ways to infiltrate the Labour party. Prospective MPs are coming under suspicion. Has this Dr Phutt of yours been behaving in any way that might suggest he's looking for vulnerabilities in our selection processes? My office has received an amber warning about him. There's an asterisk by his name.'

'Selection processes? *Amber warning?* But an asterisk's good, isn't it? You told me the one by my name indicated I was reliable!'

'Unfortunately, the asterisk can't be taken at face value; it's multi-purpose and context-specific. In the context of an amber warning it's a red flag indicating *potential national security risk*. Has there been a check on his credentials?'

'No, not formally.' Lancing looked askance. 'Is this really *a problem*? I mean, *potential national security risk* is rather vague, isn't it?'

'Apparently *potential* has the potential to be raised to *verified*. Only *suspected* lies between. Unofficially, in our business, nuance and suggestion sometimes have the credence of verifiable fact.'

'How can that be? Aren't decisions—'

'The thought doing the rounds is that Phutt could be working for the Chinese government… or for the Taiwanese.' He cleared his throat apologetically. 'Or, *possibly*, a double agent working for both. It's been noted that he collects single malts. That's a *very* expensive hobby. There are a number of internet memes with the persistence of crypto originating from sources tangential to him aiming to undermine our belief in the trappings of culture and our sense of the civilised self. We fear there's some sort of attempt going on to weaponise them.'

'Goodness, how would that work?'

'We don't know, dear boy, we don't know! But if Dr Phutt mentions Confucian Study Centres it may be that they hold the key.'

'Vivien did say he mentioned something called the Sino-UK Friendship League.'

'*Interesting!*' said the Chief Whip cryptically.

Lancing recalled his wife's opinion of Dr Phutt. 'She thinks he's prone to the injustices of empire.'

The Chief Whip grimaced. 'Ah, yes! And we the industry of bad conscience!'

'She devoted her Saturday evening to him. She thought his conversational gambits a wee bit extreme.' Lancing was finding the situation increasingly uncomfortable. 'Do you want me to sack him? He's come all the way from Bangkok!'

'No, no!' He smiled a ghoulish smile. 'That might be too hasty. Nevertheless, we cannot let scallywags get away with things, can we? He might well attempt something when you're in the Far East. Why don't you see if you can catch him out trying to recruit someone to infiltrate our party organisation?'

'But most of the members of my delegation are Tories.'

'Yes, that won't do; we're not helping them. Look, you'll think of something. When he's on home turf he'll get sloppy and reveal for whom he's batting.'

Meekly, Lancing nodded, the nod signalling that he agreed with what he didn't fully understand and about which he was disinclined to enquire further for fear of being painted a fool. He thought the Chief Whip's worldview was too improper to be ironic yet consistent with a desire to baffle.

'Another thing, while we're having a nice chat. This film you're encouraging.'

'Yes, *The Knowledge Factory*. I'm not altogether sure I'm—'

'Word's come down from on high that we need to avoid being too Left-leaning.'

'Really? But why? After all, we are the party of the Left.'

'Well, this documentary-making couple you're talking to might be over the line; more Left than Consensus Left. They've been seen fraternising with our Socialist Worker brethren. They've a habit of joining protest marches and spend their weekends weaving banners. Those who are experts in such things are concerned their banners are unusually incisive.'

'I see.' Lancing knew little of the arts and crafts but he was pretty certain banners were not woven.

Rather grandly the Chief Whip was ready to sum up. 'What is called for is *a watching brief*! We're keeping an eye out for you so carry on as normal.' He then added, in his most deadpan, chilling voice, '"*See it, Say it, Sorted!*"'

As Lancing might have foreseen, the grandees in the parliamentary tearooms were muttering his name over their tea and scones: 'Ah, young Lancing! A bit of a polarising character, is he not? Too much initiative being expended in the wrong directions?'

'You can't run with the Bean-Counters and hunt with the Creatives. It's bound to turn bloody.'

'I hear he's in bed with Tory *arrivistes* for non-political reasons. *Ill-judged!*'

'Indeed! It's a taint! Very ill-judged!'

TWENTY-SIX

That same morning Conquest's first task, in a day full of meetings, was to join Professor Newell in the senior common room to greet Dr Phutt. He was accompanied by Tommy Ballantyne, the university's Director of Finance.

Professor Newell was the essence of formality. 'Ah, here comes Professor Conquest, our Vice-Chancellor. Vice-Chancellor may I introduce Dr Phutt?'

'Good morning, Malcolm. Dr Phutt, a pleasure to meet you at last.'

Newell beamed while they shook hands.

'Our Director of Finance, Mr Ballantyne.'

'Delighted.'

'Dr Phutt has a very busy day ahead of him, Vice-Chancellor. They're expecting him at Portcullis House to assist with the arrangements for your visit to the Far East, but he wanted to come here first and say hello.'

'Well, Dr Phutt, very generous of you to find the time! We're very impressed by the help your organisation is giving us with our recruitment in the Far East.'

'I am very happy to be here – my first time in your beautiful country – and have this experience of your diversity, of your university and see your parliamentary system in operation. It will afford me many worthwhile lessons.'

'Your hotel is comfortable?'

'Yes, I was there last night. For the weekend I was with Mr and Mrs Lancing in their beautiful constituency home.

Thought provoking! They say travel broadens the mind; well, my mind has been contorted into many new shapes already and I only arrived *Friday evening!*'

They all laughed with appropriate gusto.

'You must excuse me if I seem over-enthusiastic but my new experiences this morning include antiquated tube system and many American franchises. Even my hotel is called Bon Jovi.'

'It's a Marriott Bonvoy,' said Newell patiently as though it wasn't the first time he'd corrected this misunderstanding.

'Your Church of England is a marvellous institution and I was very happy to experience it at first hand yesterday. No hand of Rome in the order of service. *Strange but very good!*'

'*Ah!* So, you're not a Christian?'

'Oh yes, Roman Catholic! I was taught by Irish missionaries at an early age. Opium of the people! Who said that? Karl Marx or Sigmund Freud? *You tell me!*' He laughed pleasantly.

Conquest thought he should direct the conversation to more practical matters. 'How long are you here?'

'Oh, just today and tomorrow. I return to Bangkok on Wednesday.'

'Very good! If I might ask,' added Conquest with slight air of hesitancy, 'what do you know of the Inside/Outside Foundation?'

'Ah, truth serum time!' Phutt laughed again, more strained this time. 'Have I been catched out? I think the Inside/Outside provocateurs have been manipulating statistics to make palm oil production seem out of control in certain South East Asian countries. It would be impolite to mention them by name – the countries, I mean – but in the courts of greenwashing offences this has created a political problem that is embarrassing many companies with an international reach. Many much-loved delicacies cannot achieve their optimal price-point without palm oil. Palm oil, salt, and sugar are foundational experiences for the modern palate. Americans love palm oil without ever realising they consume it! When the population of Saudi Arabia has doubled in size you will see what I mean.'

'Are you saying,' asked Ballantyne ponderously, with his usual sharp eye for a socio-economic political scandal, 'this is seen as meddling in the sovereign concerns of certain states?'

'All I say is that many COP delegates are invested in palm oil and they do not like their status as eco-warriors disturbed. They do not ride about on bicycles in clothes made from recycled plastic bottles *for nothing*! Social media is the new village pump and, of course, the new water cooler.'

The three academics exchanged glances, unsure what to make of Dr Phutt's response to Conquest's question. The latter's instinct was to be soothing.

'I can see you have things on your mind. In mentioning the Foundation I didn't mean to upset you.'

'Europe jangles the nerves when you arrive,' Phutt said, semi-apologetic. 'The First World is the new Third World.'

Shortly he left for Portcullis House in the company of Professor Newell.

'Not exactly forthcoming, was he? The journey seems to have unsettled him,' decided Ballantyne.

'Yes, he did seem somewhat upset. A bit prone to exaggeration, I'd say. Was he being evasive, do you think?'

Ballantyne gave a mystified grunt.

TWENTY-SEVEN

Conquest studied the middle-aged couple sitting before him. They looked principled but pummelled by adversity. The man had the introspective demeanour of a repressed fanatic; she – undoubtedly the producer of the pair – was a touch blowsy but had the look of someone who could be ruthlessly efficient. *A formidable team*, he thought. Fine if they were on your side, but if not, *watch out*!

'We cannot believe,' she was saying with studied indignation, 'that Marcus Lancing won't have universities exposed for poor performance, even though he's a member of the opposition! It's neutering societal investigation!'

Conquest knew he was required to defend Lancing, even if half-heartedly. 'Well, the political considerations loom large.'

'He's saying tuition fees are a no-go area; student suicides, definitely not. Are these really *political* issues?'

Conquest was aware that no serious attempt at suicide troubled the reputation of his university, but still he felt obliged to disagree. 'Well, I'm not sure that being a member of the opposition party necessarily means one should be critical of what universities are doing. Circumstances are difficult, you know!'

The man made a series of grunting noises that suggested disgust.

'We think,' said she, seemingly interpreting her partner's grunts, 'that these kind of preconditions speak of the increasingly hobbled circumstances that documentary film makers – *and journalists in general* – have to put up with. Not only are these preconditions of his a bar to honest reporting, the BBC has *also* informed us it has certain guidelines it requires us to follow.'

'Oh?'

'We have to conform to the guidelines of the "*Our BBC*" initiative, apparently!'

'What sort of guidelines are those?' wondered Conquest.

'It wants us to represent universities as "*Our Universities*". It's a fraternal issue; it sees universities as kindred organisations, "shackled in the shadow of the state". I'm not quoting the Director General, you understand! We were aware the BBC had well-developed guidelines about diversity and community representation within its ranks, and in its output taken as a whole, but now our executive producers are telling us the same must be applied in any in-depth study of Higher Education. What they won't stand for is our series giving the impression universities aren't for everyone.'

'I see. So you're talking about an inclusivity issue, I suppose?'

'Yes. Mind you, it's not a level playingfield! The Corporation has specific conventions about how politicians should be questioned so they don't come over inappropriately.'

Conquest was not inclined to sugar his response. 'You mean so none come over looking ignorant, arrogant or stupid?'

'Yes, although nobody would use judgmental words like those.'

He now grasped what she was driving at. 'I see! They won't allow you to apply the same principle to universities! As it's a documentary about "*Our Universities*", you're required to have a quota of gormless students saying cretinous things rather than everyone being bright and intelligent?'

'I wouldn't put it like that... but there is an access imperative, and there has to be a human face to grade inflation.'

Conquest scratched the back of his head furiously. 'So, one of your focuses is the human dimension of grade inflation?'

'No, we see grade inflation as primarily statistical; we don't want to be sociological but rather have individual human issues as our focus.'

Conquest didn't know what to make of what he was hearing but had an increasingly strong conviction he didn't want his university involved in their plans. 'Look, whoever told you this stuff must have been joking, surely? I mean...' He was lost for words.

'Well, perhaps you could advise us: what is this fictional version of the university we are supposed to portray?' she snapped.

'Are you aware that I have a book about to come out on the university of the future?'

'We are aware,' she said waspishly.

'My interest is the New University – *the Thinking Machine* – and I'm interested in promoting my views on its behalf. It would not help me if my present university, half-finished thing that it is, were subjected to the kind of scrutiny you have in mind. I'm willing to speak for myself, but as far as your series is concerned I suggest it would be really most appropriate for you to find a suitable subject from the Russell Group of universities.'

'Oh, we're only here because Marcus Lancing insisted we come and seek your advice. They won't admit it, but our executive producers at the BBC have already vetoed using your university because of the strangled animals issue.'

'*Strangled animals issue!* For goodness sake, no animal has been strangled on my watch!' said Conquest indignantly, disguising his immense sense of relief that the BBC had saved him with its veto.

TWENTY-EIGHT

The documentary filmmakers had hardly left when the phone rang. It was Brendan Glendale, Marcus Lancing's Chief Parliamentary Researcher.

'*Brendan*,' demanded Conquest before the other had time to speak, 'is Marcus throwing me to the lions over this Evening Standard story?'

'I wouldn't say that. *No!* He was quite amused when I showed it to him. However, I see on your website that a Professor Linkage is giving this year's Fred Bartholomew Memorial Lecture.'

The way he said it set him on edge. 'Is there a problem?'

'I was vetting his book over the weekend: *The First And The Last: A Socio-Anthropological Study Of The Unspoken.*'

For a moment Conquest was a little putout that Glendale was calling to discuss Linkage's book rather than his own. 'Ah, yes, I've just acquired a copy.'

'I gather it's quite influential. Pity he had to propose that some people are racist at the level of aesthetics. That's really not on.'

Conquest took a moment to assimilate what Glendale was saying. '*What?* Are you serious?'

'Well, I found this footnote to one of the annexes in which he revisits some of the key terms in the main text and discusses collateral branches of thought worthy of further research. Quite obscure.'

'Do I understand you suspect nobody's yet read this annex, except you?'

'Apparently not; the footnote certainly. At least that's to judge by the reviews from all kinds of respectable academics; establishment *literati* too. And the footnote's quite long, in the manner of a speculation about beauty – "beauty and the eye of the beholder", and all that sort of thing – and probably not many people have felt the need to read the annex, never mind the footnote. After all, the main text is considered challenging enough. But once this gets out I suspect there'll be trouble.' He said this with more than the usual deadpan menace. 'I mean, your Students' Union for one… and *everyone* will be culpable. You're in danger of a class cancelling.'

Conquest' quailed. 'I'm frankly a little incredulous. *What was* the publisher thinking? It's a university press, is it not?'

'Yes. Quite an editorial blip! You could get in first by cancelling his lecture.'

'Good grief, but it's already been advertised! What about the book?'

'Best if someone disowned it publicly.'

'*What, us?*'

'Why not? It would show contrition, in case contrition is called for.'

This was too much for Conquest. 'I'm already showing contrition for suggesting putting a goat in a cement mixer on the fourth plinth!'

'Yes, I thought your denial of actual intent quoted in yesterday's *Observer* was ingenious: defiant but pliant. We could use your skills over here! I hope you're not saying you've run out of contrition?'

'I do feel there's a limit, Brendan. Otherwise I'm in danger of coming out as a self-obsessed crybaby.'

'Fear not, Clifford, public abjection continues to trend, so my crowd-sourcing sources tell me.'

'From what you say it sounds as if Linkage's remark is rather difficult to find, and it might be best if it stays buried.' Conquest said this stiffly, defiant of the other's scaremongering.

'Well, no, we can't risk the wrong sort of controversy, not concerning your university, or Higher Education. Given your present difficulties, your institution needs to be without blemish.'

'Wherever this comes from, Brendan, it's most unwelcome!' After a few moments thought Conquest added, 'And before doing anything I think it would be prudent for me to speak to Marcus.'

'Ah yes, that reminds me of the other reason why I've called! Marcus is calling the first meeting of his All-Party Parliamentary Group this evening, the ones going to the Far East in his delegation. He'd like the non-parliamentary delegates, like yourself, to be there, although the goat thing means I'm not sure it's wise for him to be seen talking to you. Would you find it too frightening; there'll be rather a lot of Tories attending?'

'No, of course I *wouldn't mind*!' said Conquest tartly, refusing to indulge Glendale's sardonic teasing. 'Is Dr Phutt with you? I understand he's supposed to be helping your team with contacts in the Far East.'

'Oh, yes, he's here all right. Being *very much* the know-all. Come tonight and bring strong drink if you have any to spare, and plenty of peanuts. I'm sure Marcus will agree: *Professor Linkage has to go!*'

'We'll discuss that when we meet,' insisted Conquest, and brusquely terminated the call before Glendale could.

Much exercised, he took up his copy of Linkage's

book to search for the offending passage. After half an hour's unsuccessful rummaging, during which he became increasingly vexed, he had Erma Radisch call in Professor Spirakis, the head of the Department of Comparative Epistemology. Once they were both seated he raised Linkage's book as if it were a species of relic.

'I've spent the last hour with this book, very much in the spirit of a general reader. I know you're partisan for Linkage and I'm wondering what *you* make of it?'

'Well, I wouldn't say... I don't know that I'm able... It's very knotty, if you know what I mean.'

'Quite! *Knotty?*'

There was a silence. Spirakis seemed at a loss to know how to start.

'But you *have* read it, haven't you?' said Conquest, alarmed by the sudden thought that he hadn't.

Spirakis's reply was hesitant. 'What makes some readers despair is Linkage's methodology. I'm by no means an expert, you understand, but he devotes the first three hundred pages to the closely-argued creation of a whole set of neologisms needed to pin down aspects of a field of theory that he argues were previously "outside language". These he regards as the building blocks of the radical methodology required to rethink the manner of political tropes that impinge on Involuntary Human Transactional Theory.'

'So, did you get through those three hundred pages?'

'In part, no,' confessed Spirakis with little show of guilt.

There was a thoughtful silence suggestive of the fact that Conquest was not greatly surprised by this admission.

'*But,*' continued Spirakis, 'I understand Linkage argues that to address the question without this preliminary work is pointless since those readers that don't will be endlessly trapped in traditional concepts that cut them off from the expanded field of thinking appropriate and essential to its consideration.'

'Yes, but what is the question?' said Conquest in some exasperation.

'Well, that's the tricky thing, identifying the question. It could be said to be: *What are the politics of Involuntary Human Transactional Theory?* But Linkage argues that that's just too neat, and expecting a one-step question and answer is another curtailment of the appropriate methodology.'

Conquest decided Spirakis's sketchy grasp of Linkage's work was licence to confess his own shortcomings as a reader. 'Well, I found the preface challenging enough. It is wonderfully obscure.'

The other reciprocated with understanding. 'As Linkage himself would admit, it's not for the general reader.'

'Are you sure the students you're bringing him in to teach aren't just wallowing in mystification?'

'I think it's more of an adventure in creative thinking.'

Conquest laughed, assuming Spirakis was being droll. The blank look on his face suggested no such thing.

'Aren't you expecting rather a lot from Linkage? Somehow it seems to me that you hanker after putting the adherents of the Dresden School to the sword. Am I mistaken?'

'I think that's a stretch,' said Spirakis, his voice strained.

'Well, if so, there's a snag, I'm afraid. I've been informed that Linkage's musings on the collateral reach of his thesis throw up at least one unfortunate aside. You may have skipped the footnoted material in the annexes but I understand there's a taint of racism hanging over one of them.'

Spirakis gulped.

Again Conquest hefted the book. 'You haven't come across such a thing, I take it? I've had a quick look, trying to find it, but I've run out of time and patience...'

Spirakis looked mortally wounded. 'If the adherents of the bloody Dresden School find it they're perfectly capable of laying a trap for Linkage.'

'My experience – brief though it is – suggests they'll have to be extremely dedicated to find it.'

'Oh, well, then I doubt they will,' muttered Spirakis disparagingly, 'they're too intellectually incurious!'

Conquest felt moved to take pity on him. 'Then perhaps it will always remain buried. I mean, after all, it's a footnote to an annex! In any case, it would be a great help if you could finish reading the thing and see if you can spot the offensive utterance. Would you do that? And if you do spot it, get back to me asap!'

Once Spirakis had gone Conquest called in Erma Radisch and asked her to find Professor Fenchcurch, Pro-Vice-Chancellor Advancement (Form & Function). As chance would have it he was in his office on the floor below and soon at the door.

'Misha, I have a task for you. I need clarity and I suspect you have the assiduity to help me achieve it.' Conquest smiled wearily at the man, who looked pink and startlingly fresh.

'Thank you, Vice-Chancellor. I must say you arouse my curiosity!'

Conquest picked up his copy of *The First And The Last: A Socio-Anthropological Study Of The Unspoken*. 'Have you seen this? It's Professor Linkage's book.'

'Ah, yes, he was here the other day, wasn't he? Rather cocksure, I thought.'

'I'm told his book is groundbreaking.'

'Really?'

'I'd like you to see whether you feel we can endorse its contents.'

'Sounds fascinating!' Fenchurch regarded the book suspiciously. 'Do you want to tell me what's amiss?'

Conquest had a different strategy in mind for his second reader. 'No... No, I'm not certain there's anything amiss. I'd like you to read it without prejudice. It's rather urgent, so I would be grateful if you could treat it as a priority. I understand there are copies in the university bookshop.'

Fenchurch took the book and turned it this way and that, examining it with a caution that was almost comical. 'May I presume to charge the purchase as an expense?'

'Quite so.'

'Then I will report back. I should have enough time this week to study it thoroughly.'

Now Professor Murray Woolworth, Pro-Vice-Chancellor, Academic Affairs, was called in. As chance would have it he too was in his office and even sooner at Conquest's door.

'I am gifting you this book,' he said as Woolworth settled on his sofa. 'It's by our Professor Linkage. I'm told there's a racial slur in it that we ought to be aware of. I'd like you to find it for me.'

Gingerly Woolworth took the proffered book. 'That is... *extremely awkward*!' He flipped the pages and looked aghast at the density of the text. 'Have you any idea where I should look?'

'I'm told it's in one of the annexes, but somebody senior in the university has to have read the whole thing to make sure we're in the clear if it comes to censuring Professor Linkage.'

'Oh dear, but we've only just invited him back!'

'Mmmm, it's tricky. I'm hoping my informant is being alarmist but we cannot risk an unintended endorsement, can we?'

'No, indeed, Vice-Chancellor. I will see to it.' He flicked through a few pages. 'Although I must say...'

'Not bedtime reading, I admit. Dense. But I expect there are compensations in there somewhere.'

When Woolworth had gone Conquest sat back, well satisfied with his afternoon's work. His trust in Brendan Glendale was minimal, and the opinions of three of his senior staff should be more than adequate cover for whatever was to come, even Glendale's apocalyptic version.

However, the readings didn't proceed quite without a hitch. Within an hour Professor Fenchurch was back.

'Vice-Chancellor, I have secured a copy of Professor Linkage's book. I've been thinking about your request, and I have a concern. You're not asking me to police this for inappropriate sentiments, are you?'

'Well, actually, Misha, I rather think I am. It's just that I would prefer you weren't primed as to what to expect.'

'Well, if it's a slur that touches on the question of *difference*... I must decline the task. There are certain things that I am not prepared to encounter.'

Conquest pondered for a moment. 'Misha, is that not to succumb to moral panic?'

'Panic is a life-saving instinct, Vice-Chancellor. To my mind, one that should be respected.'

'Nevertheless, Misha, I'm afraid I must insist. I believe this task falls squarely within your remit as Pro-Vice-Chancellor Advancement (Form & Function), and in the present circumstances your discernment and knowledge make you indispensable.'

TWENTY-NINE

In a distant part of the Houses of Parliament there was a large notice on the door of a committee room. It read: PRIVATE MEETING. *The All-Party Parliamentary Group's Enquiry into the Social, Financial and Educational Issues Consequent on International Recruitment in Higher Education.*

Despite the notice's size, it was the sound that led Conquest to the venue. His heart beat faster as he opened the door. The noise was deafening. The room was thronged with short, misshapen men. They were drinking as they talked: with tremendous, misguided intent.

'Ah, Professor Conquest! Good evening to you!'

Brendan Glendale was just inside the door. He had a guest list on a clipboard and was in the act of vigorously crossing out Conquest's name. He looked unsteady on his feet and his voice was noticeably slurred.

'There's the intellectual brainpower of a small light bulb in this room so I expect you'll find the company to your taste. Let me introduce you to someone you don't know and have no desire to meet. How about Ron Leadbeater, MP for Lesser Grantchester, the incumbent of the last Liberal Democrat seat in Southern England. Or perhaps we should join the several Tory Re-Introductionists anxious to be out of the country for a while. They're lurking by the gin bottle discussing the logistics of multi-cultural conscription.'

'Brendan,' said Conquest, somewhat appalled, 'how much have you had to drink?'

'*I drink to forget.* Who said that?'

'I have no idea. Putting this All-party Parliamentary Group together is your greatest triumph and you're going to mess it up if anyone notices!'

'You're *so* right! Marcus couldn't have done it without me.'

'I think you ought to go somewhere quiet and sober up.' Conquest felt uncomfortable at revealing his concerned side to somebody as supercilious as Glendale. After all, he'd never had anything approaching a kind word from him. What he feared, from the expression on his face, was that he was about to launch into a tearful confession about something to which he had no desire to be privy.

'My dog—'

'Brendan, I *do not* want to hear about your dog. Where's Marcus?'

'He's not here yet; he's talking to Janet Street. They're hatching a plot to cut me down to size. Marcus thinks I keep a diary so he won't talk to me anymore. It's his new thing. He keeps joining committees, important oversight committees, and he won't tell me what's going on. It's ridiculous when I write his position papers and make sure his ideas have currency. Little thanks I get!'

At this Conquest's doubts about what might be going on in Lancing's office without his knowledge came to the fore. 'They're not policy statements, I hope.' He gazed at him sternly. 'Are they?'

'No, but I have to keep him in the public eye. They're positive speculations as an encouragement to thought and debate. My job title should be *Special Parliamentary Advisor*!'

'When he comes I'm going to get him to send you home.'

'Have you heard? Your Dr Phutt is causing *consternation*. He's been classified as a national security risk!'

'*What?* Don't be ridiculous! Where's this come from?'

'Oh, you know, can't say; need to know basis only. We spent the day with him working on the delegation's itinerary. He's not doing anything I couldn't do and we had to put up with Special Branch listening in. He's been flagged up. They think he might be looking for someone he can compromise.'

'Has Marcus heard about this?'

'Yes, he's been informed, but it's a secret.' He put his finger to his lips in a theatrical gesture commanding silence.

In disgust, Conquest began to steer him towards the door but he resisted, reversing the grip on his arm.

'Did you know,' Glendale confided, 'we're seeking Organisation Designation Authorisation so we can veto our own projects?'

'No,' said Conquest grimly. 'I didn't.'

'Have you noticed, a bar of soap starts out too big; it has only one moment when it fits the hand perfectly. Alas, then the moment is gone: too small, then smaller and smaller, provoking existential thoughts about the passing of all things. A soap dispenser, on the other hand, gives the illusion of stasis, permanence; a pleasant illusion until the very last pump.'

'Yes, very philosophical.'

'Come and meet the Re-Introductionists from the other side of the Chamber. The chief plank of their political programme is a root and branch return to Cold War politics. Their proposals for private members' bills include the reintroduction of identity cards, national service and dog licences. They'll be entertained to meet someone with an allegiance to an MP they considered highly dangerous. The political psychologists in their ranks have identified Marcus as an autodidact with a tendency to flight of thought. Not that their opinions meet much acceptance, here or anywhere!'

To humour him, Conquest let Glendale propel him towards a knot of portly men dressed in brightly coloured striped blazers of the kind to be seen on a summer's day at Lord's cricket ground.

'Hello, hello, who do we have here?' crowed one of the group as Glendale insinuated himself into their midst.

'It's Master Lancing's bottle washer,' said another. 'I do love a good bottle washer!'

'I bring you Professor Conquest,' announced Glendale with a decidedly camp flourish, 'Vice-Chancellor of University London Central, educational activist and influencer!'

'Clive Winston,' said one of their number, holding out his hand and shaking Conquest's. 'You're a member of Marcus Lancing's circus too, are you, Vice-Chancellor? You must be the delegation's university insider. Welcome aboard.' He then reeled off the names of his four companions: 'Harry, Mustafa, Fritz and Javier. Gentlemen, meet an *actual* vice-chancellor, *Professor Conquest*!'

There was a general hubbub of greetings. Conquest realised they were disposed to be friendly. Somehow Glendale, he noticed, had slipped away. Left to his own devices he was uncertain what to say. Then he blurted out what was on his mind. 'It's said the advisor to our delegation, Dr Phutt, is a national security risk.'

That caused a good deal of merriment. 'Excuse the laughter,' confided Clive Winston, 'but it seems to have been forgotten that Dr Phutt was outed by our Far East Research Group years ago. I suppose he's still working to sabotage Western cultural values?'

Conquest was taken aback at substance being given to Glendale's claim. 'This must be a mistake! He's CEO of a student recruitment agency called *Intercontinental Global Collegiate Colleagues United.*'

'And five years ago he was running one called *International Collegiate Colleagues Universal*. Every few years a new company; same mission, name passing similar to sow confusion.'

'Marcus flew him over to advise on who our delegation should meet in the Far East. Isn't he supposed to be at this meeting?'

'Maybe he's been detained.'

'I'm sure Marcus will vouch for him. He had him down in Kent for the weekend.'

'Domestic vetting, I suppose. Not likely to reveal very much. The problem is the powers-that-be never show themselves.'

Conquest was still trying to grasp the implications of what he was saying. 'The powers-that-be?' he said with a frown. 'They being?'

'Well,' said Clive Winston, nodding to the others, who clearly knew what he was going to say, 'informed opinion has it that it's the Inside/Outside Foundation, but we know the Inside/Outside Foundation is beholden to other entities.'

Harry, Mustafa, Fritz and Javier bobbed their heads and smiled knowingly.

Conquest was beginning to suspect that together they were heading down the rabbit hole. 'Ah,' he said, 'the think tank nobody's ever heard of with connections to secret political associations! *Entities?* And what entities might those be? They're not deposed royalty and their advisors, are they?'

'It's a Russian doll with a fuzz ball in the middle.' Winston cupped his hands to demonstrate. 'We think we know, but we haven't any proof! Anonymous off-shore accounts, dead letter drops.'

Conquest was provoked enough to verge on rudeness. 'Well, where's the conspiracy? Why all the cloak-and-dagger? I mean, it's nothing more than a student recruitment agency, surely?'

'No, no, it's an *organ of cognitive warfare*!'

It was all so *very* good-natured but Conquest was becoming increasingly impatient and about to forego politeness completely unless someone furnished a compelling explanation.

'It's become clear in the past year or so,' confided Winston, 'that the Chinese are making a detailed map of the UK's universities. We believe their intention is to identify all meaningful scientific and cultural activities with the aim, medium-term, of undermining them. That's what we mean by cognitive warfare.'

Conquest was amused and incredulous. 'How are they going to do that?'

'By habituating universities to international recruitment as a significant source of income. The view of the Chinese state is that the optimal Chinese population in any of our university departments is one capable of facilitating the transfer to their own education system everything the state apparatus deems useful. Once that process is completed the British hosts will be subjected to a sudden withdrawal of demand. Whole universities and important research departments, only sustainable because of international income, will experience catastrophic economic collapse leading to redundancies, amalgamations, closures, loss of research staff to Gulf States and so forth, exacerbated by the resourcefulness of the administrative class in protecting its own.'

The latter point occasioned a faint, grim smile from Conquest.

'What's more, this attack on our universities is only part of a bigger strategy. The twofold Chinese aims are, first, the wholesale transfer of technical and scientific excellence and, second, the undermining of any culturally-specific activity that sustains the ethical basis of post-Enlightenment identity politics, which the Chinese loathe because identity politics, in turn, sustains the idea of difference at the level of the individual.'

Conquest was embarrassed. This, he recognised, was a Hermetic Conviction Narrative, and it was in the nature of Hermetic Conviction Narratives that they were irrefutable. A glance at the others showed him that none shared his scepticism. Rather they were nodding their heads sagely in silent accord. It was clear there was no point in arguing. 'Er, is this grounds for an emerging governmental policy?' he asked, skillfully masking his feelings.

'No, not yet. We have many still to convince.'

There was a general murmur of assent, also indicative, in its minor notes, of disgust at the idiotic, purblind refusal of some of their Tory colleagues not to take the threat seriously.

From the distance came the booming of Big Ben; it was eight o'clock. There was a loud appeal for quiet. At the other end of the committee room Lancing, newly arrived, was the centre of attention. He now addressed the delegates, reminding them why they were there: the inaugural meeting of *the All-Party Parliamentary Group's Enquiry into the Social, Financial and Educational Issues Consequent on International Recruitment in Higher Education.* His end of the room was laid out in a hollow square of tables. In response to his call to order the delegates drained their glasses and without haste began to wend their way towards their seats.

As far as Conquest was concerned the meeting was a disappointment: apart from some suitably stirring opening remarks from Lancing it was little more than a briefing about the delegation's proposed itinerary in the Far East, and an exhortation to read the disclaimer documentation prepared by the parliamentary legal office. There was one passing reference to Dr Phutt and no sign of him.

When the meeting was over Clive Winston took him aside. 'We hear your book is going to be rather a paradigm shifter. *Quite important!* We like the Thinking Machine chapter.'

Conquest bridled. 'You can't have read it, it's still being printed!'

'True, I haven't; I don't read, but it seems unauthorised copies are in circulation. We're just not sure that you're backing the right side, sticking with Lancing. Your libertarian instincts make us think you'd be more at home in our ranks. We're the ones trying to halt the social depredations of politics. There are going to be some very good seats at the next general election with thumping majorities! Esteemed senior managers from the public sector *always* welcome!' He elbowed Conquest gently under the ribs and winked before walking away.

Just then Marcus Lancing appeared at Conquest's side. 'I have been tearing my hair out trying to reach you,' he said.

'Those men leaving the room right now are...?' Conquest nodded pointedly.

'Ah, Tory Re-Introductionists. They're as mad as hatters, but I suppose you might say they're true blue Conservatives. They espouse national discipline.'

'I think they're conspiracy theorists. *"Cognative warfare!"* And one of them just propositioned me.'

They both laughed heartily.

'Look,' said Lancing suddenly earnest, 'what's with this liquidizing fuss in the Press? Have you got it under control.'

'Yes, it's all nonsense. Five-minute wonder. Nothing to worry about.'

'Good. You gave me a fright.'

'But your filmmakers have cried off. Apparently the BBC told them my university isn't a suitable subject.'

'I heard. Outrageous, but perfectly understandable.'

'A reputation for mistreating animals is going to follow me the rest of my days,' confessed Conquest ruefully.

'I suppose they have the licence fee holders to think of. I'm not sure *I* should be seen with you. Let's go to Ways & Means. I've just been elected a member.'

Lancing called for a cab and soon they were on their way.

'Civility in all things, Clifford,' exclaimed Lancing as a large Mercedes emitting muffled rhythmic thumpings overtook them as they drove up Whitehall. 'We'll never have civility on the roads while the occupants of vehicles hide behind tinted glass.'

In the welcome dark of the taxi Conquest sank into the passive state Lancing's habit of soliloquizing induced. He was, he thought, nothing but a listening post for his latest ideas. It seemed that as long as he didn't protest too much Lancing believed he might be on to something.

'Tinted glass is an abomination suited to none but drug lords and people smugglers.' As they passed Trafalgar Square Lancing turned his gaze on the lions. 'The point is we've got about ten percent of the population holding everyone else to ransom with anti-social behaviour. I think we need a broader definition of coercive behaviour that takes a negative view of ideology. Really, there's something quite ugly about conviction when it's sustained by a cohesive set of ideas.'

Conquest grimaced, his faced turned to the side window of the taxi.

Lancing had something else on his mind. 'Now, your university could undertake some disinterested research for my all-party parliamentary group, couldn't it?'

'Research?'

'I hear on the grapevine that an All-Party Parliamentary Group has made a successful funding application for a research project in collaboration with a university not so very far from you.' At this Lancing's face creased in a meaningful way as if to say, *You know which university I mean.* 'Anyway, I think it would be an excellent idea if we had one the same: say five years for a ground-breaking piece of research. A research project gives an All-Party Group a sense of authority and gravitas. Thick, with plenty of annexes.' He smiled delightedly at the thought.

'To get funding from a research council you'd need a thorough-going outline of what your research project would seek to discover... or resolve,' responded Conquest, trying to maintain an air of academic seriousness.

'Brenda, my research assistant'll knock something up. Brenda's been servicing us long enough and I'm sure could draft something some of your research folks could work with, not that I have feelings about the idea, either way. What I do have feelings about is legacy.'

'Really? *Legacy?*'

'Yes, what I need *you* to think about is legacy. There's too much inconsequential legacy about and we have to make sure our sort isn't that sort.'

'Right, legacy. *But Brenda?* I haven't met her have I?'

'Yes, Brenda.' He did a double take. 'Oh, sorry, I mean *Brendan*. Brendan Glendale.'

Conquest felt tattered. It had already been a long

week and it was still only Monday. 'Why did you call him Brenda?'

'Oh, it was a slip of the tongue. I suppose because everyone in my office calls him Brenda.'

'Isn't that rather strange, *inappropriate*? I mean, he calls himself Brendan, doesn't he? Isn't it the sort of thing someone else might find troubling... not to say objectionable? Some kind of – *I don't know* – an egregious example of workplace harassment, hostile working environment, making fun of him and so on?'

Lancing looked nonplussed. 'I hadn't thought about it like that. It's more a slip of the tongue sort of thing.' He stared off into the distance for the moment as though contemplating an imponderable. 'I can certainly see it from your point of view now you mention it.'

There was a long silence as the taxi made slow progress in heavy traffic.

'Maybe,' said Conquest finally, 'it's been having more of an effect than you realise. He seems to be going off the rails. You need to talk to him.'

'What do you mean? I *do* talk to him.'

'About the stuff that appears on-line in your name?'

'*Yes!* I talk to Brendan, as I've already said.'

'All the position papers and discussion documents that emerge from your office? I mean, they're written by Brendan and his team on your behalf, aren't they?'

'He knows he has to keep me in the public eye, otherwise all my work is pointless!'

'This evening he'd been drinking and was complaining about the way you treat him. Perhaps you're asking too much of him.'

'What did he say?'

'He talked about soap.' He made a small, disgruntled

gesture. 'Do you really expect him to draft a research project for our parliamentary group?'

'Yes, yes! He's good at that sort of thing.'

Conquest thought it unlikely that a research project that would satisfy the Arts and Humanities Research Council could be 'knocked up' by Brendan in the manner Lancing seemed to be implying. The magnificent complacency of Lancing's pronouncements was increasingly irritating and he had an urge to say something brutal by way of a rebuke. Instead he said, 'You might let me see a first draft and I could give some feedback on the specifics. I'm sure I could put you onto some experts once I have an idea what it is you want. Has Brendan told you about Professor Linkage and his book?'

'Ah, yes, *the thing*! That could be another unwelcome blot rather too close to you for comfort! Surely your university could supply a definitive opinion on it, couldn't it? I rather feel it's something on which we all need guidance.'

'Since you ask, I've arranged for three of my most senior academics to read it and report back. Has Brendan shown you the offending passage?'

'No, he hasn't. I don't have time to read these days, not books with arguments and footnotes. Briefings and digests are my kind of thing.'

Conquest gave a wry laugh. 'You're not the first MP who's said that to me this evening. So, Brendan is the only one who's seen this remark?' He felt reservations were definitely in order if Brendan was the sole source for the story.

Their taxi had glided to a halt at the entrance to the grubby alley wherein lay The Megatherium members club, also known as Ways & Means. Lancing paid off the fare and they made their way to the sitting room on the first floor.

'Confidentially, Cliff, I've got a bit of a problem. That Dr Phutt you introduced me to as a liaison person in the Far East seems to be not what he is, *at all*!'

'Ah, yes, I'm not surprised you say that. Brendan reckons he's a national security risk.'

'*Potential* national security risk; just *potential*!'

'Those MPs I was talking to also seem to know. They said something about him working to destabilise our universities and sabotage Western cultural values.'

'*Really?* Well, nobody takes them seriously. Still, it's not good news for me if it gets out.'

'I was expecting him to be at the meeting.'

'Me too. He shot off after lunch, according to Brendan. Some idea about contacts for my delegation to meet out in the Far East. He's back with Brendan tomorrow. Look, Cliff, my wife is an expert in risk and she's identified him as high risk with very little reward. High risk/low reward is not a good place to be. Vivien says he's got some theory about the Eurovision Song Contest and cultural abjection. I'm not sure it's very positive for us Europeans.'

'Have you noticed: *everybody's* got *a thing* about *the Eurovision Song Contest?*'

'Vivien says that, according to Phutt, the Chinese believe it represents the nadir of the spectacle in the era of experiential commodity fetishism. After that there's nothing but the void.'

'Really?'

'Yes, seems so. I think we'll have to ditch him once my delegation's back in the UK. What about you?'

'Ah,' Conquest vaguely waved his hand in the air, not wanting to commit himself to anything, 'watching brief. If it proves to be that he's part of a Chinese effort to destroy the British universities I suppose I'll have to drop him... but he's an invaluable help with our international recruitment.'

Ignoring the possibility of irony, Lancing moved on, eager to discuss more congenial things. '*Now look,*' he said forcefully, 'in order to make my University of the Wealds and Wolds into something more tangible I need to announce you as my choice for its first vice-chancellor. Since I put the idea to you I've taken advice from our Concept Team at Scribbling Inc; they seem very positive on the idea.'

'Despite the goat and goldfish business?'

'Yes! I was surprised too. Actually, it seems to have made your name there. It's one of those counter-intuitive, visibility things I don't really understand. I'm actually rather envious!'

Conquest had been wondering whether Lancing had really meant it when first he had proposed the idea of him taking on his brainchild. Now it had been mentioned again he wasn't sure whether he felt cornered or flattered. His doubts were considerable. He still hadn't seen enough to suggest the idea had real substance. Was it anything other than one of Lancing's madcap enthusiasms? 'To be frank,' he said with some caution, 'I think I'd like to see some more detail. A new university's an exciting prospect, but I would prefer it if there were a little more flesh on the bones of the thing before you asked me to decide.'

'Sure. When Dr Phutt's gone back to Bangkok, *Brendan*—' he looked at Conquest meaningfully, stressing the use of the correct name – 'will be able to put the whole team back onto their work with Scribbling Inc's Concept Team. The Press like solid things like names they can research, so in the meantime I'll just put your name about a bit. Get the feeding frenzy primed. Oh, and speaking of Scribbling Inc, I've arranged with Mrs Bakehouse for someone to come and see you tomorrow morning to brief you about the Inside/Outside Foundation.'

THIRTY

The following morning Conquest spent a pleasant half hour with a cup of coffee before Erma Radisch appeared at his door to announce the arrival of Alex Slocum, Senior Future Officer of Scribbling Inc.

Slocum had the pallor of someone who spent his working life in meeting rooms and libraries. Silver grey, almost white hair, at the back neatly trimmed just below his collar and at the front swept composedly across his forehead. He was dressed in the style of a senior academic at an institution where status was assured by hallowed tradition: sober, old-fashioned, but stylishly so. All-and-all an unexpected look for an adolescent in glasses who seemed, to Conquest's jaundiced eye, about seventeen. Apart from the clothes, little about him suggested a person commanding respect for his opinions, able to meet with politicians and diplomats on an equal footing, something guaranteed by his magisterial work on the interactions of the institutions of world order and their tribulations.

Conquest's appraisal was swift. He made up his mind to give him short shrift if he strayed from delivering anything other than a simple message.

'I've come,' said the youth, 'at the behest,' he continued in his carefully modulated voice, 'of an esteemed colleague, to give you some advice about the Inside/Outside Foundation. It seems you've got yourself caught in the tentacles of a boa constrictor.'

'A boa constrictor is a snake,' objected Conquest.

The boy smiled whimsically. 'Our – *my* – boa constrictor is a figure of speech, not an actuality. At Scribbling Inc our mission is to re-define and embellish The Real in pursuit of *enjoyfulness*.'

It was Conquest's turn to be amused. Was his laugh appreciative, or was it a sardonic imitation of appreciativeness? Even he was not sure.

'The point is, I'm afraid the Inside/Outside Foundation is actually a bit too much of a mouthful for you to swallow.'

Conquest looked the boy up and down blankly and then, with a certain degree of caution, said, 'Let's sit down shall we? And take this one step at a time. Would you care for some coffee?'

'Coffee? No thank you. But if you want some I'd be happy to join you.'

'Maybe in a while.'

They sat.

'You were saying about me swallowing the Inside/Outside Foundation?'

'Yes. Universities can, of course, become umbrella organisations, taking specialist entities under their wings, but University London Central would find the Inside/Outside Foundation a big fish in its small pond. More than you could chew, if you follow my meaning?'

'I'm sorry, that was a bit of a metaphoric jumble,' decided Conquest, wondering why he was apologizing, 'and you seem to be misinformed. I have no desire to do anything with it. I want to know *what it is*!'

The boy frowned, took off his glasses, inspected them, and returned them to his ears. 'I was told something entirely different. I was told you were proposing to incorporate it as the political outreach and civic education unit of your university.'

The extent of the misunderstanding startled Conquest. '*As what?*'

'Well, what it would provide is international excellence and an upping of your general standing in the Global Institutional Opinion Formers ratings; an antidote to the decline in values that characterises the British Higher Education system. However, University London Central, if you don't mind me saying so, is rather an insignificant university as these things go. Naturally, the Inside/Outside Foundation has to be very chary about its relationship with any university.'

Conquest had been hastily gathering his thoughts during this strange, boyish apparition's speech and was sufficiently piqued to want to defend the standing of his university. 'The point is, the Inside/Outside Foundation already seems to have a significant relationship with my university, piggybacking on our international recruitment effort, so we would seem to have already passed some significance test or other, *wouldn't we*? What's more, I don't understand the role Scribbling Inc is playing here. Do I understand you've been sent by Mrs Bakehouse to act as some kind of intermediary?'

'To be candid for a moment,' said the youth with the utmost earnestness, 'what Scribbling Inc is interested in is *you*! What we want to know is whether your book is as revolutionary as we've been told it is. If it is, we have something to talk about. If it isn't, we haven't. We've heard great, exciting things about it and if they're true we'd like to use your expertise. Scribbling Inc would, of course, be willing to pay a proportionate consultancy fee and retainer.'

'Use my expertise for *what?*'

'Well, we seek someone with a Higher Education background to lobby for some of the educational causes we espouse. Don't you argue that men have dinosaur brains?'

Conquest was indignant. 'No, I certainly do *not*!'

'I've been informed there's a chapter in your book about educating dinosaur brains!'

'No, not at all!'

'Isn't it the case that you've dissolved the entire edifice of the university into an audio-visual fintech soup? Aren't students to receive life-skills passports rather than degrees? Don't you propose that universities be re-cast as part of the experience economy, with study centres as the new norm serviced by neural networks?'

The mention of study centres was the final straw. 'This is pure speculation! My book is still being printed and only three people have read it in draft! At the root of my arguments,' he added, thinking that what he was about to say was going to sound extremely humdrum compared to his description, 'is the belief that informed interdisciplinarity calls for strong disciplines!'

'I expect it leaked. Everything leaks these days. It's called "backwardation", one of our industry's buzzier buzzwords.'

Conquest knew backwardation had nothing to do with leaks, but he couldn't recall what backwardation did actually mean. 'So, is that the basis for Scribbling Inc wanting me to act as a lobbyist for the educational causes it espouses? If so, I don't believe we have the grounds for any such cooperation.'

'Ha ha! I'm sorry if you think I'm being too combative in testing you out. At Scribbling Inc we value shortcuts to interpersonal intensification, although there's an absolute prohibition on the tropes of bullying. We believe in the soft power playbook and are laser-focused on duty of care. That said, we seek the frontiers of dynamogenesis! If I may, I'd like to give you a glimpse of the Bigger Picture as we see it.

'Interested parties in conjunction with Scribbling Inc plan to reboot charity as self-interest. Why? Because the psychological damage of displacement is a *post-partum* given. We also need to rid the country of the on-going trauma of smart motorways and gonzo healthcare, just as we're determined not to return to the back-stabbing, stack-a-pleb mentality of the past. We who have visited Legoland have glimpsed the future of social housing! The new sculpture trail is ecological heritage! By turning the bloodlust of psychopaths into something that's accepted as part of everyday business practices we believe we can fundamentally reduce sexual predator behaviour in social settings, particularly from authority figures such as priests, politicians, civil servants and police officers. You may not know this but as things stand sexual predators rate very highly on the contentment scale. That has to change! We want to own multiculturalism and empower diversity, not just pay lip-service to them. We are entering a Darwinian historical phase so let's be brave and say "Yes!", it's time to say "Maybe" to the stormtroopers of Christian Aid and channelise the politically incorrect; time for a black Mona Lisa and for Porgy And Bess with an all-white cast. And universal unisex mothering for all! We believe in your untested potential! We owe it to ourselves for the sake of future generations to work on our neuroplasticity. What we champion is free radicals: the opinion-makers of the future.'

Conquest was certain "free radical" was a term misplaced from chemistry. 'We might as well be discussing the life-skills of vampires!' he said with the utmost cordiality.

'Ha ha ha! That's an extremely good line. Mind if I make a note of it?' The youth reached for a pen and notebook from his rucksack. 'Useful, I can assure you,' he said as he jotted it down, 'when caught short on the wilder shores of the person business. We want to own you because in the shifting allegiances of the House of Commons there are those who would value your contribution in their larger efforts. You are, in a phrase, "being courted". Your remark about a goat and a cement mixer on the fourth plinth was somewhat controversial but being satirical about contemporary art goes down well with serious-minded folk. It's been good for your people's person branding. We're beginning to think it would be a definite positive and in everyone's interest, including your own, if you were a controversial figure, *provided...*' Here he paused meaningfully... 'those around you are seen to be solid and reliable. This could be a sliding door moment for you. *Happy days!*'

Conquest looked at him with a calculating, quizzical eye wondering what to make of the boy wonder and his hyperbole. 'You see,' he said, 'my problem is that when I get close to a source of supposedly reliable information about the Inside/Outside Foundation what I find is some sort of questionable belief in the cultural significance of the Eurovision Song Contest.'

'*Questionable?* No, no! We see the Eurovision Song Contest as a paradigm of inclusive intercultural collaboration. It has an element of competition but, unlike the Olympic Games, competition is sublimated into song. No yellow cards, no red cards, just the green card of *enjoyfulness*.'

His smile grated. As far as Conquest was concerned it was inexplicable. 'I'm sorry,' he said, 'but Marcus Lancing seems to have completely misinformed you about my request to him!'

'Ah, yes, Marcus Lancing! He's the epitome of the modern politician who disavows conviction, but we all love the things he foregrounds, don't we? They're levelling. It's a cliché to say levelling down is the new levelling up, but common sense should tell us that, *truly*, levelling down is the only way to satisfy the grass roots. "Dilution Politics", we call it. It's culturally acceptable to all those not beguiled by the misty promises of Albion. Unfortunately, it's bound to be accompanied by selective multiplicity – the postcode lottery – otherwise the government can't sustain public services; it's a finance thing. The fact is, we think you should come out in opposition to Lancing's plans for the University of the Wealds and Wolds.'

'*What?*'

'On environmental grounds.'

'*Environmental grounds?*'

'Hundred of miles of access roads, underground padel courts, postgraduate courses for wilderness survivalists and set-aside reservations for wilding instead of grouse shooting! Have you heard about his call for English Heritage to embrace the earth latrine? In the leafy suburbs these are policies, are they not?'

'Well, to be charitable I'd say they're "wonkisms".'

'And to cap it all he's in bad odour at the moment over his cat-licensing gaff: *lost his touch*!'

Conquest was mystified. 'Cat-licensing gaff? What's that?'

'He's threatening cat ownership by promoting a pet licensing policy.'

The thought of Lancing being caught out by one of his rambles exasperated Conquest. 'Look, he doesn't do policies; he's not that kind of politician.'

'He's litmus paper for Millennials. They don't care for policies, or politics but he's disappointed them; they expect velvet revolutions with grandstand seats and sweet'n'salty nibbles on the side.'

'*Hang on,* you say Marcus is in trouble because he's said cat ownership should be licenced but the goat in the cement mixer business has enhanced *my* people's person branding! Surely, in an animal loving democracy that doesn't make sense?'

'We like controversy, but not toxicity. Toxicity is a debit on the nation's emotional bank account. Pet licensing is toxic. Goat shredding, on the other hand, suggests a certain novelty of outlook that goes down well on Planet Metro. All it needs from you is a little push and he'll be a goner. He'll be sitting on the backbenches with the other sad Blondin donkeys. If the Anti-Testosterone League has its way he'll have the party whip withdrawn.'

Conquest laughed uneasily. 'You want me to stab him in the back?' Even as he said it he felt a twinge of gratitude that at least the boyish ruffian was offering him a way of extricating himself from the morass that the University of the Wealds and Wolds might easily become. '*Really?*'

'Since he has nominated you to be the first vice-chancellor your voice would be heard in all the right places. The adult in the room needs to say, "No!" We'll provide you with a comprehensive unfeasibility study.'

'But I thought Scribbling Inc had a Concept Team working for Marcus on the University of the Wealds and Wolds?'

'We do, but now, as our Forward Thinking Brand Ambassador, he's working *for us*. More importantly, we're working for Conservative party interests that want the National Parks left alone. You see, for every Concept Team we have a Counter-Concept Team – it's part of our proof of concept procedure – and as our Environmental Advocate Academic you would trump his Forward Thinking Brand Ambassador.'

'The thing is,' decided Conquest finally, 'you talk exactly like he does!'

'You can hit the ground running, or go to the back of the queue,' said the boy wonder. 'We can hit the ground running or we're at the back of the queue. We are where the rubber hits the road! POMO for FOMO!'

When he had gone Conquest pondered his parting remarks. It was beginning to feel as if everyone around him was speaking the same post-industrial management argot.

POMO for FOMO?

His conclusion was that the intention behind the boy wonder's visit had been to co-opt him while at the same time maintaining, as far as possible, an air of uncertainty around the real purpose of the Inside/Outside Foundation. What it had inadvertently done was to suggest that there might be some truth in the Hermetic Conviction Narrative he had heard from the Re-Introductionists; that the Foundation's sponsors wanted to subvert, by insidious means, the lineaments of liberal, democratic, Western society. He recalled that when Bostik Snr had first talked to him he had mentioned the Foundation having "a public relations off-shoot' that was "definitely very active". It now came to him, not for the first time, that that off-shoot might be Scribbling Inc.

Later still, he realised he had thought of himself as Labour by conviction; now he wasn't so sure. Creeping over him he was beginning to feel Lancing's desire to be agnostic. As for betraying him over the University of the Wealds and Wolds, well, that would be an absurdly suitable act of treachery.

While he was still pondering all this, Erma Radisch informed him that Professor Fenchcurch, Pro-Vice-Chancellor Advancement (Form & Function) had phoned from his office and wanted to see him on an urgent matter. Ten minutes later he tottered in having spent the night speed-reading *The First And The Last: A Socio-Anthropological Study Of The Unspoken*. Conquest was impressed. He hadn't expected any of his readers to report back – even with concerns – for at least a week.

Fenchurch looked drained, stubbly and his copy of Linkage's book bristled with sticky coloured tabs.

'I thought it best to report...'

'Yes! This remark you're concerned about, Misha?'

'It's more than a remark, Vice-Chancellor, it's an attitude, an outlook, a deep-seated prejudice.' Fenchurch flicked feverishly through the pages of the book, nodding his head hypnotically. 'Ah, here it is! This is one of his quotes: "Blonde had me hate the dark ones. If I can I will. If I cannot, all unwilling I will love them still". D'you see?'

'Not entirely. Where is this?'

'At the foot of page 527.'

'*Oh dear!* You know what, I'm afraid I've given my copy to Professor Woolworth? Did I hear you say it's a quote?'

'You did.'

'From where?'

'It's graffiti from the wall of a brothel in Pompeii.'

Conquest was momentarily bewildered. '*Pompeii?* Meaning what? Meaning Linkage has quoted it from *another book*? A book about...?'

'Archaeology, Vice-Chancellor. Yes, seems so. It's footnoted.'

'What, the footnote is footnoted?'

'No, it's a two page parenthesis. It seems the intention is to discuss the role of the witchhunt in the politics of Involuntary Human Transactional Theory.'

'So I take it that this quote is part of a larger argument.'
'Oh yes, indeed!'
'I see! And it's a taint... or isn't it?'
'Yes, a taint. I suppose so. It's a pretext; an underhanded way of uttering racist sentiments by attributing them to others.'
'Then we should... What *should* we do about it?'
'Call it out! Vigorous censure and dismissal!'
'What, strip him of his emeritus professorship?'
'I should think so, wouldn't you?'
'I don't know, Misha. I need greater visibility. Have you read the whole thing?'
'No, not yet. I thought I should report back as soon as—'
'Yes, yes, quite right, but this is not what my attention was first drawn to. You need to continue. At the very least I'll have to consult Lord N'Garbi, chair of Senate, before taking any action. Perhaps you could provide me with photocopies of all relevant passages?'

Professor Fenchurch rose to his feet as though heading for the photocopier that minute. 'A point needs to be made, Vice-Chancellor, a point *must be made*!'

THIRTY-ONE

The Chief Whip was a picture of disapproval. 'Look here, Lancing, it was only yesterday I was offering you a way out of your troubles. Now what do I find? I've had to call you in because you've been digging a deeper hole for yourself! It's doing the rounds in a very public way that you're advocating that multiple cat ownership should be taxed. Pet licences are *not* Labour policy! There are reactionary forces on the other side of the House proposing the re-introduction of dog licences, and even *thinking* about cat licences is way off beam. The great British pet-loving public won't stand for it. It's box office poison.'

'Don't you mean ballot box poison?' muttered Lancing rebelliously. He should have been cowed by the Chief Whip's displeasure but he was becoming increasingly fed up with the seeming ease with which untruths were being attached to his name.

'Whichever...!' said the Chief Whip ungraciously. 'What's more the was-Royals have dropped you from your protection duties at Royal Ascot. They won't touch you with a bargepole now you've been outed as pet-averse. In their circles you're about as welcome as a Prussian pimp! The fact is I've been asked to put the frighteners on you.'

Lancing sighed deeply. 'I cannot deny that I spoke – *in haste*, *off the record* – about such a condition being required of a certain member of my constituency. It was not a policy statement it was an... an *outburst*!'

'Pets are only second to innocent children in the eyes of the British public. It's rumoured the Tory's dog licensing proposal has a clause banning extendable dog leads! Typical Tory constraint on human rights!'

'Constraint on canine rights, surely?' muttered Lancing, still in fractious mood.

'Let's not resort to cleverness, Lancing. Your recent pronouncements on revolutionising the National Parks have made you particularly visible when, in fact, it might have been more prudent to be invisible while we quantify the threats being made against you. Turning vicars against you is careless, and now this! I fear there will be repercussions; cats are a delicate subject.'

'Funny you should mention my visibility. I've been working up an enhancement of my public visibility concerning the hiking trails of the Isle of Thanet. Sort of thing popular in the early evening on BBC Two.'

'No, Lancing, *no!*' The Chief Whip made a show of extreme patience. 'You have too many ideas about yourself! You have to understand that once you've reached the threshold of public visibility anything you say is construed as policy. I've seen the report of your remarks to the Thanet Tomato Growers' Association in the Margate People's Gazette. Not only did they reek of policies, they smacked of evangelising! Let's be clear, the Commentariat is on your tail; someone from the Press is monitoring your every utterance! Are you aware of how many charities concerned with the welfare of cats there are out there?'

'I can't say I am.'

'Ninety-nine and counting! The vigilantes of the People's Alliance for the Protection of Cat Charities Lottery are about to make things very hot for you. Don't forget, these things ricochet round social media, particularly the Therapeutic Felines For Bridge-Playing Widows constituency.'

'*People's Alliance...?* Isn't it about time the Charities Commission consolidated all these charities into a more efficient charitable system?'

'There you go again! A rich eco-system of charities is a significant contributor to the nation's political wellbeing. As for your idea of enhancing your visibility, the People's Alliance's "Turn Off Your Telly" fatwas are immensely successful. The Producers at the BBC won't touch you once they hear that you're the subject of one. You, my friend, are in danger of creating an amalgam of formidable foes! My advice is, step back, don the dishdasha and disappear to the Far East with your delegation.'

'The thing is,' said Lancing stubbornly, 'I asked my research team to find out how many dogs there are in the UK and how many tins of dog food they consume in a year.' For a moment he looked wild-eyed. 'Did you know there are over twelve million dogs in the UK? Pets are responsible for a huge amount of environmental damage. We have to find alternative companion animals. Discounting pigs, the only answer is humans.'

'Human are not the least companionable, I'm afraid,' decided the Chief Whip. 'Even so, none of this environmental moralising is reason for going against party policy and bringing up the licensing of cats... or dogs! If this goes as I think it will you're going to have to step back from your shadow cabinet duties. Self-serving opinions are an electoral hazard and you've flaunted the principle of collective responsibility!'

'*Step back?* Surely, you wouldn't expect me to resign over something so inconsequential?'

'Did I say resign? Step back is something else.'

'Really? I don't see how!'

'Step back is a form of words; resignation is a fact.'

The remark sufficiently muddied the issue for Lancing to deflate. 'It still seems rather drastic.'

'Another thing: Professor Conquest of University London Central. One of your chums! This cat licensing hoo-ha is certainly reason for you to avoid any association with *him*. His enthusiasm for shocking the public sensibility with his liquidizing animals bent is causing a tremendous fuss amongst the Whitehall influencers.'

'Oh dear! He assures me it's all nonsense.'

'Yes, I'm sure it's just a publicity stunt but – *really!* – ill-judged! It's not wise to be seen in the company of people like that. Cruelty to animals is a no-go.'

But I've been putting it about that he's my candidate for the first vice-chancellorship of the University of the Wealds and Wolds!'

'In the circumstances of you stepping back I'm afraid making any such announcement would be beyond your pay grade. Not on, Lancing!'

'And he's a member of my delegation to the Far East.'

The Chief Whip paused for thought before responding. 'Yes, perhaps that's for the best. Get both of you out of the way while the fuss dies down!'

'Well, before you decide on anything, I've been thinking about what you said.'

'Said...? *When?*'

'Yesterday.'

'About what?'

'About getting Dr Phutt to reveal himself as an agent working against British interests when my delegation is in the Far East.'

'Yes?'

'Well, once you've fast-tracked Professor Conquest as a prospective Labour parliamentary candidate, I trap Dr Phutt trying to recruit him as an operative for the Chinese.'

'You...? *You want me...?*' The Chief Whip looked positively dazed. 'Once I've *fast-tracked...*!'

It was a triumph. It was quite plain from the look on the Chief Whip's face that Lancing had, at least for the moment, turned the tables on him. 'That's right,' said Lancing meekly. 'After all, it's your idea and surely you could do a little groundwork before we leave for the Far East? Professor Conquest's a perfectly good candidate and I'm certain you can find a constituency party that will adopt him, especially if it's only temporarily.'

'Would he be willing?'

'Of course; he has political ambitions.'

It was such an obvious fulfillment of the Chief Whip's idea, so obviously sound that, despite the grandeur of his position, he could not but agree to be the enabler of Lancing's plan. 'But listen, Lancing, it'll be much the best if you keep our little deception to yourself. You understand me?'

'Of course!' agreed Lancing meekly. 'But in that case, for the moment, you wouldn't want me to tell Professor Conquest he's no longer the prospective first vice-chancellor of the University of the Wealds and Wolds, *would you?*'

THIRTY-TWO

Events had crowded in on Conquest since the news story about the liquidized goldfish artwork had first entertained London's commuters. Resuming his meeting with Professor Newell, the Pro-Vice-Chancellor (International Outreach) and pinning him down about the full extent of what he was up to in the Far East had had to wait. Tommy Ballantyne, his Director of Finance, remained wedded to the idea that there was an immigration racket at the back of it. He was even now making a five-year analysis of which departments and courses had recruited the most international students. If there was a racket, he reasoned, some admissions tutors must be in on it. Conquest was sceptical, still having a lingering faith in Professor Newell's shining sincerity. However, the Chinese conspiracy theory he had heard from the Re-Introductionists had been playing on his mind and he had asked Ballantyne what the consequences of a sudden loss of income from international students would be. Ballantyne had pulled a face and said, 'Dire'.

Erma Radisch had been instructed to hold his telephone calls. He had a moment of tranquility while he waited for his director of international recruitment to arrive. He took up the University of the Wealds and Wolds Unfeasibility Study newly arrived from Scribbling Inc. The speed with which it had arrived following his meeting with Slocum, their Senior Future Officer, made him realise that copies were most likely already in circulation somewhere in Whitehall. Across the title page was emblazoned 'For Your Eyes Only'. An accompanying note informed him that to conform with privacy legislation Marcus Lancing was identified as 'Subject A'. The opening line of the introduction ran: 'An ecological disaster is about to unfold in our National Parks'. Conquest felt a prickle of discomfort at the back of his neck. Was it a premonition of disaster? Possibly, but whose? He fanned through the Unfeasability Study. It was almost an inch thick. He didn't doubt it was a thorough assassination job on the University of the Wealds and Wolds; the environmental case unassailable. Never mind that Scribbling Inc had been assisting those concerned with Higher Education in the Shadow Cabinet to develop the idea. It was clear that for every positive the Concept Team had developed a Counter-Concept Team had simultaneously been at work turning it into a negative.

With a sigh, Conquest tossed the Unfeasibility Study onto the coffee table before him. He hardly had time to move to his desk and open his email account before Erma crept in silent as a ghost: 'There's a man here from the Irish Embassy.'

'Irish Embassy?' A look of concern crossed Conquest's face. 'Not Professor Newell?'

She looked at him blankly, shaking her head.

'What's his name?'

'Captain Blackward.' She held out his card.

Beneath the crest Conquest read: "Captain Iain Blackward, Senior Diplomatic Intelligence Officer, Republic of Ireland". Rather awed, he sensed that what was to come required reinforcements. 'Will you find Professor Woolworth and ask him to join us. Don't let this man Blackward in until he's here. Say I'm occupied right now.' Conquest indicated with a silent nod of his head that she should go and do his bidding.

Blackward was finally admitted some ten minutes later, Professor Woolworth having arrived as a rather breathless bulwark against misadventure. When the preliminaries had been dispensed with and they were seated, Captain Blackward spoke.

'I believe that a Dr Phutt is an associate of yours. Do I have that correct?'

Conquest was guarded. 'If you mean of this university, then yes.'

'He's taken refuge in the Irish Embassy.'

'You must be mistaken! He's on his way to Heathrow right now!'

'He claims he's in danger of assassination.'

Conquest exchanged a look with Woolworth. '*Assassination?* By whom?'

Blackward shifted uncomfortably in his seat. 'That's not entirely clear. He's claiming political asylum.'

'I'm sorry? *In Ireland?*'

'He's requested the protection of the EU.'

Conquest felt a twinge of indignation. 'You mean he's decided our protection isn't good enough? Surely there aren't forces at large here wanting to assassinate him?'

'Again, as things stand nothing is entirely clear. Since he has an association with your university my office thought you should be informed in the hope you might be able to help us achieve some clarity. Dr Phutt wants certainty from our side without being entirely forthright on his.'

'You know he is here at the invitation of the MP Marcus Lancing?'

'We do. In EU circles Marcus Lancing is a well-respected green campaigner and my government has no wish for this matter to escalate into a diplomatic incident involving him.'

Blackward's estimation of Lancing's reputation in EU circles caused Conquest some surprise and suppressed merriment. 'I was unaware of the extent of his international reach,' he said.

'I understand he's always been suitably alarmed about leaving the EU.'

'Well, I'm sure he'll be suitably alarmed to hear about Dr Phutt! I'm not certain I should be telling you this, but I was recently informed the British authorities consider Dr Phutt a national security risk.'

Blackward pursed his lips but was otherwise unmoved by the news. 'I'd have to take that on advisement. He claims he's a political dissident. Any idea why he's thought to be a risk to national security?'

'It seems to be something to do with the activities of the Inside/Outside Foundation. Have you heard of it at all?'

'Doesn't it train football pundits for FIFA?'

'Referees, I think you mean. And sniffer dogs for police work. Seemingly, these kinds of activities are a cover for its real purpose, which is to undermine Western cultural values, particularly to degrade the university system. Dr Phutt could be an operative of the Foundation, perhaps a turncoat; I have no idea which.'

'I see,' said Blackward noncommittally.

'If the latter were the case he could have made some powerful enemies, something hardly compatible with our view of him as a support for student recruitment.'

'Student recruitment *would seem* an innocent enough activity. I checked our SCRT notifications before coming and it seems he was in Baku in 2018 and Damascus twice the following year.'

Conquest pursed his lips in an expression of profound thoughtfulness, his mind a blank as to what visits to Baku and Damascus might mean to the other man. 'Student recruitment fairs?' he offered.

'Possibly. We've asked for a clarification. It's only a matter of time before the Americans get interested in this and then there'll be fireworks. Why did Mr Lancing invite Dr Phutt here?'

'Marcus wanted to commission him to provide introductions to governmental bodies in the Far East interested in empowering international educational cooperation at university level.'

'Really?' Blackward said this dryly in a manner that suggested disbelief. 'I understand Mr Lancing lobbies for Scribbling Inc, which is owned, via a shell company, by the Obamas.'

'*Obamas?* No, that can't be right. NBA in Africa is Obama, isn't it? At one time I did wonder if Chinese interests might be funding it through the Inside/Outside Foundation, but now I think it unlikely. Have you heard of the Eurovision Song Contest? Apparently, Scribbling Inc endorses it as a model of ethical cultural collaboration. Contrary to that, it seems the Inside/Outside Foundation, and the Chinese, wish to encourage it as an expression of Western decadence.'

'Murky!' exclaimed the unfortunate Captain. 'On the whole, do you think you could come and collect Dr Phutt? Confidentially, we've been advised we shouldn't touch him with a barge pole. If you could persuade him to drop his request we'd be most appreciative. You'll find him in the buttery at the embassy.'

As Captain Blackward concluded his goodbyes, Erma Radisch poked her head round the door.

'Excuse me, Vice-Chancellor, Professor Newell's here,' she said. 'He's been waiting for his appointment with you. Shall I send him away?'

Conquest shook his head. He indicated she should show Blackward out and let the other in. Professor Newell ambled in without delay and collapsed comfortably into the place on the sofa to which Conquest directed him. He immediately engaged Woolworth with a question about the well being of his dahlias.

'*Malcolm!*' interrupted Conquest, his tone sufficiently brusque to halt their exchange. 'There are a number of inconsistencies that you and I need to address together. How are you, by the way?'

Professor Newell sat up, a picture of attentiveness. 'Fair, Vice-Chancellor, very fair.'

'Good! Your friend, Dr Phutt, is currently in the buttery at the Irish Embassy.'

A slight frown of concern crossed Newell's face. 'Is there something amiss?'

'He thinks someone's trying to kill him.'

'*Goodness!* Surely some mistake?'

'He's asked for political asylum, apparently. Tell me, do other universities have the same relationship with his company that we do? I mean, is there something special about our relationship with him that no other university has?'

'Well...' Newell hesitated '...two of his sons studied here in the Department of Mathematics. Your predecessor arranged something of a special deal for him. I think it was a sort of one-off thing.' The admission was somewhat shamefaced as if he was well aware the arrangement was questionable.

'An incentive, perhaps. Nothing as crude as a bribe?'

'Yes, quite. The police aren't involved, are they?'

'Not yet.' Conquest's mind was racing. 'Now, listen. I am going to go to the embassy and persuade him to take a taxi to the airport. We need to get him out of the country. You two stay here. Furthermore, Murray,' he continued, turning to Professor Woolworth, 'while I'm gone, *Murray*, would you please do me the great favour of discovering what POMO for FOMO means!'

THIRTY-THREE

Marcus Lancing's senior colleague, Jeff Deal, the Shadow Secretary of State for Higher Education, peered about him gloomily. 'Unfortunately, your blue sky thinking turns out to be not what I had in mind, Marcus.'

'I thought you loved the University of The Wealds and Wolds.'

'I do. I did. It's one of those great ideas that isn't meant to be, like the leaning tower of Pisa.'

'Didn't we undertake to future proof the landscape, Jeff?'

'We did, Marcus, but the fact is, you can't make a university carbon-neutral. The decarbonisation auditors must have tried it twenty different ways. I've even had my kids trying. Just don't talk to me about carbon off-set. I should never have stopped teaching GCSE chemistry.' He groaned and put his head in his hands. 'Beyond my second divorce I see nothing ahead but the road to perdition.'

'It's not that bad. And I hear there's a resort in Mexico wants to see our plans.'

'But it still won't cut it on a crowded island, I'm afraid.'

'What about fighting for legacy, Jeff?'

'These days a successful political career doesn't even warrant a marble bust. Not that anybody knows how to make them anymore.'

'No, I mean, we should stick with the dream of crags and moors, and students uplifted by their surroundings. Isn't it a vision worth fighting for?'

You fight for it, old cock, I'm booking a Thai massage for the crick in my neck. As I see it, Marcus, they want you to leave Higher Education alone for a while. There's a rumour they're going to get Alex Waist to fill in for you. He's a rising star, apparently. If you want my advice, I'd kick off to the Far East with your delegation. They won't demote you while you're out of the country. The Press would see it as bloody-minded, vindictive in-fighting. We don't do that in Labour.'

The harsh laughter that followed was quite disturbing.

THIRTY-FOUR

Should Labour's Chief Whip require information, his secretariat could provide detailed files on every Member of the House, their staff and their relations with other significant persons. It did not take long to discover who had brought Professor Conquest to Marcus Lancing's attention and proposed him as a member of his advisory committee on Higher Education. It was the influential Labour peer, Lord N'Garbi. The Chief Whip was wary, knowing that Lord N'Garbi had a long history of acting as an advisor and mouthpiece for Chinese interests. Nevertheless, without delay he went to call on him in his office. They stood at the open window smoking cigars.

'This senior academic you recommended to one of my MPs, Lancing of Thanet Channel? Name of Conquest, Clifford Conquest. Know who I mean?'

'Ah yes, Professor Conquest!' N'Garbi was a big man. The cloth of his lounge suit would have dressed two ordinary men. His face consisted of a strange assortment of over-large features that gave him the imperious look of a debauched Roman Emperor, yet he spoke, persuasively, almost hypnotically, with a certain refinement. 'Perfectly nice man, the iron fist, when necessary, knows how to employ it.'

'You recommended him so I suppose...'

'Yes, I chair Senate at his university, University London Central. Good man, watched him carefully. A coming man.'

'What about this goat mincing business on the Fourth Plinth?'

N'Garbi laughed indulgently. 'Exchanged messages with him; he assures me it was a typical university set-up: malcontents. Universities chock-a-block with them. More to the point he's been putting, very successfully, a badly holed ship back on an even keel. Certainly, I recommended him to the member for Thanet Channel. Thought he was in need of a little steadying. He behaving himself?'

'Started well, but perhaps got a bit ahead of himself.'

'There's been rumblings amongst the Big Beasts about some of his off-the-cuff pronouncements. Cat licensing! Not best pleased. Ever occurred to you that he might be a little mad?'

'Can't say it has, but now you mention it…' The Chief Whip tossed the idea aside as unproductive, there being too many MPs of whom the same could be asked. 'A little hyperactive, well-meaning, stirred the pot once too often. Probably heading for a spell on the backbenches to cool down a bit. The reason I've come asking about Conquest is that it's been suggested we should consider him as a parliamentary candidate. What d'you think?'

N'Garbi squeezed his lower lip meditatively. 'I wasn't aware his political ambitions were so widely known! We have talked about this. There are worse ideas. He's not young and impressionable, and he has scruples. I suppose all that tells against him. Trade unions wouldn't like him either; strayed too far from his roots. Suit a city with couple of universities though. Got somewhere in mind?'

'Not as such. Would you be prepared to endorse him?'

'Of course, if I'm asked.'

'Could you canvas the idea about a bit, see if it stirs up anything malodorous?'

'Certainly. Come to think of it, I have some friends in the West looking for someone solid and reliable.' He nodded his head thoughtfully, warming to the idea. 'Might be a good match! Leave it with me, why don't you?'

Their cigars were coming to an end, as was their conversation. N'Garbi took in the other man shrewdly.

'On another front, while you're here, how is facing down the forces hostile to the integration of China into the First World order going these days?'

'Tories very excitable. Us not so much.'

'I'm relying on you having your finger on the Party's pulse. Tours of North Sea wind farms are very popular. We've the biggest cruise liner yet coming this way. I want to be sure it gets a welcome from the Press.'

'You know how it is, Franj. I'm afraid that as long as there are members of the Politburo Standing Committee making daft pronouncements there'll be a veto on most things, especially architectural salvage. It was bad enough taking all our industrial gubbins, taking the buildings as well is deemed a step too far at the moment.'

'Pity, east of Kashgar, permanent industrial revolution heritage experiences are all the rage.'

THIRTY-FIVE

It wasn't until Conquest was on the steps of the Irish Embassy that finally he got through to Lancing. Lancing spoke at a rush before he could say anything.

'We have trouble, Cliff. I'm in danger of losing my post in the shadow cabinet. We need to leave the country now!'

Conquest was not to be put off. 'Marcus, something really odd is going on with Dr Phutt.'

'Really? What d'you mean?'

'Well, is *he* aware he's been labelled a national security risk? He's trying to defect to Ireland.'

'That's awkward!'

'Apparently he's received death threats.'

'He's not the only one. I received one last weekend in my constituency. It was nailed to the front door of my house!'

'*Nailed?* That's shocking!'

'Well, no, not nailed, it was stuck in the crack, you know, between the door and the frame. "You, the ungodly who have offended against His Word will burn in the flames of righteousness" sort of thing.'

'Ah, religious nutcase! That hardly counts as a death threat, does it?'

'Well, I certainly felt threatened and intimidated. Who's threatening Phutt? He's only been here since last Friday and, surely, we're the only ones who know he's here?'

'I've no idea. Has he lived up to your expectations and done everything he was supposed to do? I thought he was meant to fly back home today?'

'Yes, yes, he is! He's been very useful. He has great contacts and he's moved things along very nicely. It seems everyone out there wants to meet us.'

'Well, he's taken refuge at the Irish Embassy, but the Irish don't want him so I'm at liberty to haul him out of there.'

'If somebody's threatening to kill him, he won't want to go, will he?'

'No, I suppose not.'

'For God's sake don't cause a fuss; it'll get in the papers. Better still, don't you deal with it; I'll send Vivien. He'll be flattered. Yes, wait for Vivien; she'll flatter him into leaving. No, better still, you leave right now and leave it to Vivien. She'll get him out of there, and out of the country. I'm in crisis here; I'll get back to you later.'

It was only as Conquest was on his way back to the university that he had a moment of recall: Lancing blurting out something about losing his post in the shadow cabinet and the two of them needing to leave the country. He was annoyed with himself for not having questioned him further because of his own concerns. Now it would have to wait, but it was, he thought, *troubling*.

THIRTY-SIX

The first person Vivien saw on entering the echoing hall of the buttery was a ratty, thin-faced man sitting at a table with a battered fiddle before him. Something told her he was an undercover security guard keeping an eye on Dr Phutt, an impression confirmed when he gave a barely perceptible nod in the direction of an alcove across the room. Vivien headed in that direction, full of purpose.

'Dr Phutt! Here you are!'

'Ah, *Vivien*! How refreshing to see you. And how unexpected!'

Vivien sat down beside him on the bench seat. 'You're meant to be on your way to Heathrow,' she said in a scolding voice. 'What *is* going on? I can't believe you're asking for political asylum.'

'I warned you at the weekend there are forces at work with evil intent in mind.'

'Yes,' she agreed reluctantly, 'I suppose you did.'

'I'm asking for the sanctuary of the Roman Catholic Church. I feel it's my best hope. Perhaps I return home via Dublin. I cannot risk anymore the public sphere here in London.'

Vivien's expression was stern, yet in a way that was kindly and full of concern. 'Why on Earth not?'

'If I say you will not believe! There is a clique close to the heart of the establishment that, for their nefarious purposes, has recruited a self-identifying psycho-sexual group from the artist-in-residence community.'

She was baffled. *'Artists-in-residence?'*

'Yes. I was told, very clearly, "they regard the staging of public outrages as a legitimate extension of their collaborative work linked to their ongoing research and exploration into the relationship between public space, architecture, state infrastructure, gender and sexual identity".' He reeled off this information with great vigour, as one does who has, at some cost, learnt it by heart. 'They call themselves the "Topsy-Turvies". Have you heard of this group?'

Vivien hadn't, but bit her lip and nodded like a conspirator. It struck her that the preposterously juvenile nature of their name gave a touch of credence, and menace, to his story.

'I was told I was to meet a fatal accident beneath the wheels of a train at South Kensington tube station. It would have been made to look like a site-specific public art intervention gone wrong, caused by the crush of school parties disembarking for the museums.'

'Ingenious! But who are the members of this "clique close to the heart of the establishment"? And why do they want you dead?'

'*Who*,' said Phutt with ferocious intensity, 'hold the power of life or death over artists-in-residence?'

'Let me think...' Vivien still had in mind Phutt's rambling exposition on Saturday evening under the influence of her Negronis. Having cancelled a full day's meetings at her husband's pleading, it was with difficulty that she was concealing her urge to drag him into the street. But however paranoid he was, she was determined to humour him. 'I'm not sure I understand. I'm afraid I don't think the Irish Embassy is going to help you just because you're a Roman Catholic.'

'Then I will wait here until the embassy closes and they will have to find me a room.'

'Your problem is that the threat is somewhat... *obscure*. Much better if we get you to Heathrow and out of the country. Where's your luggage?'

Phutt was still locked in confessional mode. 'Unfortunately, I accidentally recorded one of them talking to their handler at the Bangkok Biennale. They receive financial incentives at such places to encourage them to turn their programmes into weapons against the rest of culture—'

'No, no,' decided Vivien firmly, 'you're leaving, going to Heathrow. I'll go with you. We'll pick up your luggage on the way. Come, your memories will be all the sweeter if we go now.'

His hotel was on Cromwell Road, ominously close to South Kensington tube station. She badgered and cajoled him, and bundled him from taxi to taxi. She was persuasive, firm and determined. Her mobile was like a live thing in her pocket. She ignored it. It was only as they hit the Hammersmith flyover that she thought to ask him, 'Who warned you you were in danger of being assassinated?'

'Brendan Glendale told me. He whispers a lot! *Whisper, whisper, whisper!* The vertical is he's hyper-informed, he really is. You should warn your husband: Brendan Glendale is not what he seems! And if he says his concerns are strictly humanitarian, *do not believe him*! It is I whose concerns are humanitarian!'

Vivien wandered the departure hall of Terminal Five deeply perplexed. She had accompanied Dr Phutt to the very limit of what was possible without a boarding card and passport. He had shed a tear as they had parted. She was relieved to have got him away but now she faced an even more urgent problem and she needed time to think. The question was: What was Brendan Glendale up to? Of all the risks that she had conceived of as harming her husband's political career, some kind of saboteur or traitor in his own team was one to which she had scarcely given a thought. It was, after all, a known and quantifiable risk, the kind for which she would have expected her husband to be on the alert. Obviously not! If ever there was a prime example of asymmetrical risk it was being betrayed by a trusted employee. And, of course, now she could see that someone who behaved like Brendan Glendale was bound to become a liability sooner or later. She recalled that when Marcus had taken him on she had dismissed his CV as AI-concocted, but seen that as nothing more sinister than a reflection of the comprehensive he had attended with a socially homogenous North London catchment area. Was now the time, she wondered, for consternation?

THIRTY-SEVEN

Professor Spirakis, the head of the Department of Comparative Epistemology, had misty, youthful memories of the annual departmental cricket match at the university where he had held his first academic appointment. It had been an anachronistic ritual then, but the afternoon's slow motion rhythms had lodged forever in his memory. There had been strawberries, pots of double cream and the families of the lecturers mingled with the students, lounging on a grassy bank. It chimed perfectly with that part of his nature drawn from his mother. She was one of the five Eastwood-Ashfield sisters and when he was a boy she had served on the local parish council. Fond memories placed cricket ineluctably in that chain of Home Counties evocations that included village choral festivals, half-timbered bus shelters and misty-eyed salutes to warm beer.

The idea that now he was in charge he should put on a departmental cricket match to mark the end of the department's examinations had come to him quite suddenly, unbidden. A cricket match, he dreamed, would be a welcome break from the polemical disputes and the factionalism of a department that was notoriously the most fractious and bloody-minded in the university.

Given the enduring nature of scholarly disputes, it can easily be imagined that, like many well-intentioned schemes, Professor Spirakis's cricket match took on a symbolic life of its own. His idea had been that the staff should play a students' eleven, but as the prospect of the contest took a grip on the department it became clear that the event was not being taken as an occasion for amicable rivalry but as an opportunity to crystallize the department's most potent schism: the Dresden School versus the Zeeland Faction. Whatever their views, let not the sincerity of the different parties be doubted! True, one or two remained on the sidelines. In particular there was a Pragmatic Realist lecturer who eschewed ideology. He quoted Walter Benjamin – "Fashion is the eternal return of the new" – and, to the scorn of the Dresdenites, pictured the ideological dispute in terms of the ten-year stylistic cycle in automobile design from rounded corners to sharp angles, and back again. He was doomed ever to be stuck on a teaching-only contract unless he recanted, but being married to a small animal vet he welcomed martyrdom.

Having marginalised and then ousted Professor Linkage and the Zeeland Faction, the adherents of the Dresden School had assumed a commanding role in the department. Inevitably, their undoing was already under way well before Professor Spirakis had sought to bring back Professor Linkage. It was brought on by the students' fading enchantment with their orthodoxy. In their heyday those they taught had seen the adherents of the Dresden School as youthful radicals forever on their side. But, alas, being lecturers with careers, the Dresdenites had persisted, endured, fathered children, sought promotion and generally become somewhat settled in their habits. The Consequence? A gap had opened up that began to look and feel to the students like a generational thing. No longer on the same wavelength, the student body at large had chosen, in a largely unspoken expression of estrangement, to throw its weight behind those clamouring for the ideological constructs of the Zeeland Faction.

That Wednesday, the day of the cricket match, was blessed by a drowsy summer's afternoon. When the adherents of the Dresden School came out onto the pitch they provided a vivid visual confirmation that a goodly percentage of the department's intellectual firepower was a self-identifying group. Professor Spirakis, observing from the sidelines, already perceived them as lean and hungry in a Cassius way, but now it was the ponytails against their whites that struck him. Despite being sculpted with the particularities of the flounces and frills of *haut couture*, a group-think could undoubtedly be discerned in their response to nature's depilation. The effect, as they tossed balls to one another, waiting for the batsmen to come to the crease, suggested a conformity equal to the way they all illustrated their scholarly texts with photographs of shopping malls and stills from Surrealist films.

Spirakis switched his gaze to the opposition and registered that its members, still donning pads and joking on the steps of the pavilion, eschewed the ponytail in all its forms. Several had requested their barber shear them like sheep in spring, most notably the region to the rear of the skull called the occipital where sprouts the last wellspring of hair capable of being nurtured as a ponytail. It was then that he noticed amongst them the laughing figure of Professor Linkage. He stiffened slightly, reminded that he had to report back to the Vice-Chancellor on the accusation of racism hanging over Linkage's book. His face was well masked by his dark glasses in the deep shade beneath the London plane tree. Here it was, he thought, the problem he had been gifted with by his pre-senile predecessor: by slow degrees Professor Blatvik's recruitment policy had resulted in an intellectual asymmetry that had left the department woefully at odds with itself. Now war was imminent, the dark clouds of strife rolling in ever thicker. Whatever the outcome of the afternoon's cricket match, the wolves were at the door, about to savage the porcine tendency.

'For good or ill,' he said to himself consolingly, 'it's a game of two halves.'

The brawl, when it came, was brief and in the first instance consisted of ungainly pulling and shoving, and then moved on to shirt-front grabbing and swiping at peaked caps. In high-spirited accord with the mood of the moment Professor Linkage brandished the cricket bat he happened to be holding. That stilled the fracas, but on its back swing it laid out senior lecturer William 'Bill' Hoskins, the department's leading exponent of the Dresden School's worldview. Whether coincidence or consequence, a cerebral aneurysm had killed him before the arrival of the ambulance.

THIRTY-EIGHT

At three o'clock that same afternoon the front doors of the Frank Brangwyn Building were thrown open to the general public. To the few listening, Professor Pomfret declared the Fine Art Final Exhibitions the finest ever. Those interested in controversy made a beeline for the basement where they were ushered, ten at a time, into the presence of Toby Bostik's site-specific installation by a pair of neophyte Bostiks. In the glass liquidizer the liquidizing paddle revolved at a speed just sufficient to keep the water moving in a circular motion. In the current thus created floated a number of slivers of carrot looking uncannily like goldfish. On the left hand wall was a second part of the installation: a large canvas painted in garish daubs that proclaimed, "FUCK ART – LET'S DANCE'. Disappointment for some, perhaps, but for those knowledgeable about such matters, it was clear that Toby Bostik was heading for a First. Upstairs in the large painting studio where the majority of those exhibiting were displaying their work, the students were already snapping open the cans of lager intended for their guests. Unregulated wine sipping had been going on for several hours. The wine may have been of indifferent quality but its effects were not to be doubted. In the celebratory atmosphere, Bacchus was set loose.

Not long after three o'clock the man of the moment, accompanied by several 'Maidens of the Revolution', made his entrance bearing a large sack of carrots just bought from a Turkish supermarket. He was deeply into the onerous task of performing the serious revolutionary, for which he was much respected by the student body. His arrival soon attracted a gathering around the table from which drinks were being dispensed. He commanded the stage with ease and his straggly beard was suitably Mephistophelian.

'Now, here's the drill, everyone.' Toby Bostik took a large carrot from the sack. 'When the fascist establishment pig starts to speak—' He gave an oink and held aloft one of the carrots – 'you all do the Bugs Bunny. *All together!* Plenty of carrots to go round!'

'Yeah!' hooted an enthusiastic sculptor.

'Excuse me, Toby!' demanded Pansy Althorpe, who was somewhat slow when it came to cultural references. 'What, *exactly,* is a Bugs Bunny?'

Bostik turned to his most favored of the 'Maidens of the Revolution', known, fortuitously, as 'Rabbit'.

'Rabbit,' he said, 'show us the Bugs Bunny. It's a cry from the depths!'

In lewd slow motion Rabbit raised the carrot to her lips and bit.

THIRTY-NINE

Vivien was not to be deflected or interrupted. 'Marcus, *what the hell* has been going on in your office?'

'My office or my eco-system, which do you mean?'

She waved his distinction aside. 'Dr Phutt was saying that Brendan Glendale warned him he was about to be assassinated. Glendale seems to have convinced him his life is in danger from people here trying to prevent him from spreading his—' she stopped as though she was at a loss to know how to describe her experience of Dr Phutt's views – 'his complete gobbledygook about a Chinese attack on Western cultural values. Just answer me this: what do you know about artists-in-residence?'

It was only with extreme reluctance that Lancing was willing to prioritise her concerns over his. '*Artists-in-residence*? I don't know *what* you mean!'

'They're like a rash, everywhere! You had one in Thanet Channel last year, didn't you? That ghastly Wat Tyler mural. The peasants' revolt in modern dress!'

Lancing gave what was almost a cry of pain. 'That was an interactive social engagement programme and considered a great success, not to mention an exemplary commitment to localism.'

'And of little consolation to those stuck in A&E! Fine, but your Brendan Glendale seems to have frightened Phutt with what he took to be a credible death threat from a gang of deviant artists-in-residence. *What is going on?*'

Lancing was exasperated. 'I cannot believe we are discussing artists-in-residence. Mine was completely legitimate; co-sponsored by the Turner Gallery in Margate.'

'Was she – it was a she, wasn't it – a member of the Topsy-Turvys?'

'Look, I'm in danger of being asked to step back from my responsibilities to Higher Education. The University of the Wealds and Wolds is about to be quashed because it's not green enough! That's my career up in flames and sunk.'

'*Jesus!* First, Marcus, let's get to the bottom of what Glendale's up to. Phutt left with a warning that's he's not what he seems. It's an insider threat you've missed! You need to think: *what is he?* And if you have no idea, who can help us find out?'

He shook his head, momentarily nonplussed. 'Cliff Conquest was going on about Brendan after my meeting with the delegation. He was implying he's a loose cannon. I didn't take much notice. It was something about soap.'

'SOAP! The Society for Open Arms Politics?'

'I'm not sure. *No*, I don't think so. The fact is all this must be something to do with Cliff Conquest. He recommended Phutt to me, and he's an insider as my choice of first vice-chancellor. The irony is,' he said, wondering what kind of reception what he was about to say would have, 'I'm planning to use him as a tethered goat to flush out Phutt as a national security risk trying to infiltrate the Party on behalf of foreign principals.'

'*What did you say?*'

'Don't misunderstand me, there's no intention of going through with selecting him as an MP. Must be a credible candidate, that's all.'

Vivien looked at him stony-faced, her eyes revealing that disbelief was a good part of her reaction. 'Do you mean to say you've been warned about Phutt officially!'

'Yes, but only *potential* national security risk. And only since the weekend. Look, Viv, I've hardly seen you since then. The Chief Whip's had an amber warning about him, and there's an asterisk by his name.'

'This is a fine mess! Marcus, you *do not* do this sort of thing. It's high-risk and unprincipled! You have an alternative, *today*! Confront Brendan or call a meeting with Professor Conquest and thrash this thing out.'

'Wait a minute.' Lancing consulted his mobile. '*Ah, yes!* At six I'm scheduled to announcing the winner of the Horowitz Painting Prize at Cliff's university.'

'Cancel!'

'No, no, I can't do that! I can't tell him what's going on but I can support his university and make sure he's on side. You should come too. You never know, we might buy a painting.'

'No, you can do it if you must. I'm going to the V&A summer party!'

FORTY

It was unheard of for Conquest to receive a mobile call from Professor Spirakis, the head of the Department of Comparative Epistemology. Its very unusualness meant he took it without hesitation.

'I've trouble here in Bexleyheath.'

'*Bexleyheath?*'

'At the sports ground we share with the Wanderers.'

'Of course, yes, sorry. What kind of trouble?'

Spirakis began a long, meandering explanation that left Conquest puzzled.

'You're saying someone's dead?'

'I'm afraid so.'

'At a cricket match?'

'Yes, with a cricket bat. Apparently it started because Bateman knocked over Professor Elkin's energy drink and he called him a "blithering" something.'

'I'm sorry, say again, *who's dead?*'

'Bill Hoskins.'

'Do I know him?'

'He's a principal lecturer in my department.'

'Good grief, a *principal lecturer*! Did he knock over the drink?'

'No, no, it seems there were barbed jibes about the Grecian foot, and whether the second toe should be longer than the first.'

'Was that before or after the drink was knocked over? I

mean, how did things escalate from a drink being knocked over to a lecturer being killed with a bat?'

'Yes, it was Professor Linkage. He was about to go in to bat.'

'*Linkage?*' The name filled Conquest with foreboding. 'I've a feeling that rather complicates matters!'

'He claims it was an accident.'

'Is there a safeguarding issue?'

'Well, there was the bat.'

'Yes, what about the bat?'

'I suppose it could be construed as a club, couldn't it?'

'But you can't play cricket without a bat! Two, actually.'

The voice on the other end of the call seemed to be fading. 'I suppose it's a matter of... *definition*.'

Conquest was exasperated by the other's havering. 'Then let's call it *an item of sports gear*, shall we, and not *a club*? *Move on!*'

Spirakis's voice picked up slightly, but still seemed troubled by the message he was delivering. 'The police have allowed him to go home. They're calling it manslaughter.'

'*The police are?*'

'Well, no, Bill Hoskins's colleagues are saying that. They're saying it was ideologically driven.'

'*Ideologically driven?* That's rather harsh! I mean, if he was going in to bat it's not unreasonable to think he didn't deliberately arm himself with a bat to kill this man Hoskins, isn't it?'

Spirakis hesitated, unsure he followed what Conquest had just said. 'They're saying it was premeditated, at the level of the unconscious, which means at the very least it was manslaughter.'

'Why would they say that?'

'Bill was the department's most prominent Dresdenite.'

'*Good God, I see!* That would be taking scholarly dispute a bit far, wouldn't it?'

'Our in-house policy analyst had been seriously considering mediation.'

'Tell your staff they're to leave the criminal distinctions to the Crown Prosecution Service, *all right?* I'm not sure our insurance covers Emeritus Professors. That's a concern! Are you coming back to the university?

'Yes, I suppose so.'

'Well, come and find me when you arrive. I'll want an up-date. In the meantime I'll get the condolences readied.' Conquest put down the phone. 'Right,' he said to himself, 'let's hope this is not a game of two halves!'

FORTY-ONE

It was hot in the flat. Max looked radiant in leggings and a tank top. She was gazing at Linkage questioningly over the rim of the mug from which she was drinking. Had circumstances been normal his reflection would have been that she was richly endowed with animal life force but regrettably, at the behest of some questing man, destined to turn into Suburban Mum, but matters being what they were, his thoughts were elsewhere.

'I did mean to hit him,' he said reflectively. 'I didn't provoke the dispute but I was thinking it would most likely clock him on the back swing. He was such a twerp. Couldn't stand the man! Come to think of it, my whole return to University London Central was intended to be nothing but scholarly revenge. But scholarly revenge isn't enough, is it? Killing him is much more satisfying than winning the academic argument. Now I suppose it's over, but at least I've achieved something real.'

Max rolled her eyes. '*Great!* In my book that *is* manslaughter, if not murder!'

She had scarcely finished speaking when the doorbell rang.

'I expect that's the police come to take me into custody.'

'Right,' said Max. 'Refresh! Time to press the restart button! Don't fucking confess!'

FORTY-TWO

The Chief Whip finally cornered Lancing in the underground corridor that links Portcullis House with the Houses of Parliament.

'Change of plan,' said the scowling ringmaster. 'Not a word to anyone; Jeff Deal's gone off his head, *seriously*! Knew it was coming. He's been self-medicating with Airwick. Contrary to commonsense, we're going to promote you to Shadow Secretary of State for Higher Education. At times like this we can't have any divisions in the ranks. Report to HQ tomorrow morning at eight for a breakfast meeting; our leader wants a few words. In your case the principal motif will be "silence is golden".'

The Chief Whip was clearly not in the mood to congratulate Lancing on his change in fortune. His next appointment called and he was about to pick up speed when he turned back in mid-step.

'By-the-by, I've just had your Chief Parliamentary Researcher, Brendan Glendale, escorted from the premises. An encrypted government device has gone missing. The spooks have identified Glendale as Willy Oshidashi, the on-line disrupter; cyber actor for goodness knows who. He's a national security risk; social media posts on the dark web!'

It took a moment for the news to sink in. 'Is that temporary, or—'

The Chief Whip was vehement. '*No!* What's more, it

turns out he's been writing speeches for the Foreign Secretary in his spare time! *A bloody disgrace!*'

'I had been told he's not what he seems.'

'Quite correct! What smart cookie told you that?'

'My wife, Vivien.'

The Chief Whip leant forward and prodded him in the chest with his index finger. 'You should listen to her more often, Lancing, *she's an asset*! Another thing: none of your staff have the clearance to work for a member of the Shadow Cabinet. Get rid! And don't go to your office. The security people are ransacking it, checking for bugs other than their own. They're looking for someone to arrest and I don't want to have to retrieve you from their clutches. You might have to move anyway; something more salubrious would be fitting, to reflect your new status. And don't forget, *eight o'clock sharp!*'

The Chief Whip threw this last instruction over his shoulder as he made to cleave his way through the pedestrian traffic, silent, menacing, forever the Great White Shark.

Lancing stood, bewildered in the to and fro bustle. '*Christ Almighty!*' he said finally. 'Time to press the restart button! A game of two halves we are in!'

FORTY-THREE

Professor Conquest looked at his watch. It was quarter past five and at half past Marcus Lancing would be joining them to award the Horowitz Painting Prize for the best student display, as voted for by the Department of Fine Art's academic staff.

'Six kids and an ailing wife!'

Conquest eyed Spirakis opaquely. The other had just thrown his hands in the air in despair. The gesture signalled his inability to decide what he thought. Conquest was in no such frame of mind. He was thinking academic freedom was what it said on the bloody tin and Emeritus Professor Linkage could easily be disowned. It had happened before and it would happen again. And on would go the quest for what academic freedom meant!

'At worst,' he said, 'we can say that the Zeeland Faction has made its point most forcefully. My advice is extremely straightforward – and I'm pretty certain our lawyers will endorse this as an instruction – *avoid all contact with Linkage*. We must let events take their course, and no hint of collusion or improper interference must impinge on that.' He looked at Spirakis with calm deliberation. 'Can you do that? You can do that, can't you?'

Grimly the other nodded his acquiescence.

'Of course, it means you're going to have to cancel the Fred Bartholomew Memorial Lecture. *Force majeure* and so forth.'

Spirakis was moved to object. 'Wouldn't cancelling it rather indicate we think Daniel Linkage guilty?'

Professor Fenchcurch, Pro-Vice-Chancellor Advancement (Form & Function), who had been a silent witness to the foregone exchange, now spoke up in support of his Vice-Chancellor. 'Let's think about it this way: when things get a little too graphic it's our responsibility to blur the awkward details. Cancellation is cauterisation, not condemnation. It's like a health warning. I see it as protecting young, vulnerable minds.'

'Thank you, Misha.' Conquest smiled in a way that suggested his lips were concealing clenched teeth. 'I think we all need a sherry, but see to the announcement, would you?' The latter was said pointedly to Spirakis. 'I shall be speaking to Lord N'Garbi about this. We'll need the full support of him and the rest of Senate if we're to get through this smoothly.'

Just then Professor Newell, the Pro-Vice-Chancellor (International Outreach), ambled in, apparently oblivious to the possibility he might be interrupting something. Conquest had invited both him and Professor Pomfret, the Head of Fine Art, to take a drink with Lancing prior to the presentation in the hope that collectively they would make a suitably impressive reception party.

'Erma seems to have gone home so I thought I should come straight in,' announced Newell, smiling sweetly. 'Your MP – Mr Lancing, I believe – is talking to students downstairs.'

Conquest suppressed a groan. 'Misha,' he said to Professor Fenchcurch, 'could I ask you to go and rescue our guest, please?'

'Quite right, Vice-Chancellor! No good ever came of politicians talking to students!' He hastened away. Conquest continued to dribble sherry into diminutive sherry glasses.

'Is Dr Phutt joining us?' enquired Newell.

Conquest couldn't believe he was not being disingenuous. He laughed bitterly. 'Ah, yes, you're unaware of his fate, aren't you? Fortunately, he's no longer with us. Escorted to Terminal Five.'

Newell looked sincerely concerned. 'I'm not sure he was very comfortable, taken out of his home environment. I got the impression he was somewhat conflicted.'

'Yes, "conflicted" is perhaps the right word for it.' Conquest took a sherry over to Newell, fixing him with a stare. 'And you had no idea he was anything but a student recruitment professional? *Never* an inkling of hidden depths?'

Newell smiled sweetly. 'Can't say I did, poor fellow.'

Just then there was a commotion from the direction of the outer office and Lancing, accompanied by Fenchurch, entered at speed.

'*Ah ha!*' exclaimed Lancing, espying the glass of sherry that Conquest was holding out to Spirakis. 'Sherry! Good! A small celebration, I've been promoted! I'm now the Shadow Secretary of State for Higher Education!'

Those present managed a smattering of applause and congratulatory noises. Conquest could scarcely credit the change in the man since last they had spoken. Then he had sounded in desperate straits about remaining in post, now good cheer prevailed *and he'd been promoted*! He whisked the sherry away from Spirakis's grasp and presented it to Lancing.

'Thoroughly deserved, Marcus. Congratulations! Were this not a formal occasion I'd be tempted to ask what happened to your predecessor. May I introduce my colleagues...?'

There followed several minutes of banter and polite inconsequentials, during which the final member of their party, Professor Pomfret, Head of Fine Art, arrived. As the banter died away and the diminutive glasses were drained he said, rather pointedly, 'I think we have a memorable cohort this year. I'm sure we're going to have a very popular winner of the Horowitz Painting Prize.'

Conquest looked at his watch. There was no reason for him to have involved himself in the business of awarding the Horowitz Painting Prize. He had offered to secure Lancing's services to present the prize when scolding Pomfret about Bostik's post-Duchampian goldfish in a liquidizer. It seemed a good idea at the time, but once the liquidizing threat had become a public controversy he would, had it not been too late to back out with dignity, have withdrawn both Lancing and himself. Now he would have to make a statesman-like joke about the whole affair when introducing Lancing; an idea he relished not at all.

'Large painting studio, first floor, Frank Brangwyn Building,' Professor Pomfret informed the gathering. 'We're going to have to hurry to be there for six!'

'Ah, no,' Conquest corrected him, 'we're having the prize-giving in the gallery.'

'But—'

'Erma and Professor Woolworth convinced me it was a more fitting setting. You know what a stickler they both are for doing things by the book. Apparently, it's a matter of atmospherics. I'm sure you'll agree, Marcus, when you see our gallery: a little gem. They're already over there seeing to things.'

Pomfret was still transfixed by the idea that the prize giving had to be in its advertised location. 'But the jurors, the prizewinner is expecting us in—'

'Don't fret, Archie, it's all arranged. The staff will be there, and Daisy Chung and her parents have already been informed. I'm sure she'll have a few gracious words to say in response to receiving the prize. Forewarned is forearmed!'

As they were crossing Ramallah Green, bordered on one side by the Frank Brangwyn Building, Lancing said, 'What's the meaning of the carrot?'

Conquest looked up and there, hanging from the front of the Frank Brangwyn Building, was a large banner emblazoned with a long orange blob with a green topknot. He was dismissive. 'A prank, I suppose.'

'Rather intriguing!'

'It's Professor Pomfret's building. I expect he can explain.'

Pomfret was at a loss. 'Blessed if I've seen it before! Are you sure it's a carrot?'

'Art radicals having a little fun,' decided Conquest. 'We mustn't keep our audience waiting.'

The gallery was a remnant of more expansive times when that part of the campus had been a Church of England ladies teacher training college. What was now the university's gallery had then been the college's chapel. Tradition had it that it had never been deconsecrated which was probably what had saved it from more utilitarian uses. The university's art collection was modest. There were several vigorous Brangwyns bequeathed by the artist. They made the works by the other British artists of the first half of the 20th Century surrounding them look somewhat bashful. The watercolours by Watts and Rossetti were regularly examined by Art History students and the rather rude etching *Four Women* by Picasso was rarely passed by without a comment or two.

The assembly was small, but appreciative. Lancing was humorous and unusually self-deprecating. Daisy Chung graciously received a token for art materials to the value of five hundred pounds.

'That went off rather well,' said Lancing as they made their way back to Keynes House. Retracing their steps across Ramallah Green they could hear the roar of many voices coming from the open windows of the Frank Brangwyn Building.

'What *is* going on there?' wondered Lancing.

'Oh,' said Conquest blandly, 'the usual end-of-year student revels.' So begins the life of a political artist, he thought.

Lancing was in a hurry to be away but Conquest managed to take him aside as he was leaving.

'I can't help but wonder about your apparent change of fortune since this morning.'

Lancing was frank. 'I know, it's surprising, but it seems I've had a stroke of luck. Jeff Deal, my superior, has had to vacate his post, so I'm the natural replacement. Frankly, I have no idea what it all means, but tomorrow morning I have an eight o'clock meeting with the boss. I'll know more then, but I imagine my delegation to the Far East might be off the table for the time being. By the way, you'll be glad to know it isn't your Dr Phutt who's the problem, it's Brendan. It turns out he is some kind of subversive, playing both ends against the middle.'

'*What?* So... he's been sacked?'

'Apparently. Possibly worse.'

Conquest gave a snort of laughter. 'Not surprised, actually. Might be good for you.'

Lancing looked rueful for a second. Then he touched Conquest on the sleeve to indicate he was about to be gone. 'I'm afraid to say,' he added, his final thought, 'it seems the University of the Wealds and Wolds is a non-starter. Sorry...

environment issues have scotched it. But, overall, I do think our *alarums and excursions* are in the past!'

Conquest watched his Uber go, overwhelmed with relief. Musing on Lancing's reference to alarums and excursions, he realised that those in the know about Professor Linkage having killed Bill Hoskins that afternoon had, by some unspoken agreement, kept the news to themselves.

On that matter, somewhat later, Conquest settled back in his chair, his phone to his ear. He had some explaining to do and expected to be some time. With a squawk the thing came alive.

'*Hello?*'

'Hello, Lord N'Garbi, it's Cliff Conquest here.'

Ten minutes later he was climbing into a cab, on his way to Lord N'Garbi's club. Another twenty minutes and he was in a secluded corner of the club with a large brandy in front of him.

'Devil of a thing, relying on telephone conversations,' said Lord N'Garbi. He was in avuncular mood. 'All right for chitchat, but most things, I always think, best done man-to-man. Now, this death, tell me again.'

Conquest repeated the story of Bill Hoskin's death as told to him by Professor Spirakis, embellished with several pithy comments about the Department of Comparative Epistemology.

Lord N'Garbi mused for a while and Conquest fortified himself from his brandy. Finally, Lord N'Garbi spoke.

'As I see it, it's an unfortunate accident. I think we agree, don't we? Didn't even happen on the university's campus. I don't buy this ideological nonsense. We politicians know opinions are lightly held these days. That's why your friend Marcus Lancing is getting on so effortlessly.'

Conquest laughed wryly. 'I'm not sure "effortlessly" is quite the word.'

'You know what I mean. Still, Shadow Secretary of State for Higher Education is no mean feat for a scatterbrain like him.'

'Drives himself hard, even if he does tend to lose his grip sometimes.'

N'Garbi response was heavily jocular. 'Yes indeed, *indefatigable*, but road holding none too good; short on down-thrust! Anyway, I hear there's been a clear out, and starting from scratch with a new team is no bad thing for him. But what about you? Your political ambitions have been noticed. It seems no lesser person than the Chief Whip is clearing the way for you.'

'*Really?* Meaning what, exactly?'

'Has it in mind that a move to the Commons might be the best place for your talents. Natural progression.'

'I'm *rather* surprised! And grateful, of course!'

'Naturally you are. It seems that being in charge of a lively institution, and having a mould-breaking attitude to Higher Education is doing you no harm. Your book being due is concentrating minds. With the election not far away a lot of our lesser lights are being required to consider their options. Retirement beckons! As a matter of fact, I've got a constituency chairman tearing his hair out at the paucity of serious candidates. How do you feel about north of Watford? Wales, as a matter of fact. Wales, but not *Welsh* Wales, of course. You'd have to stand against a bunch of loonies, but the education movement is quite strong there.'

FORTY-FOUR

Marcus Lancing's tumultuous day was finally done. He brooded over his glass of wine: Brendan Glendale summarily dismissed, the rest of his staff dispersed to the offices of less exalted MPs. Word had come down from on high that he was to shun all contact with Brendan. Now he was gone, he missed the buzz of his constant texts and emails. He was suddenly singular and at a loss. Vivien, for once, was a little dazzled by the turn of events. She urged retrenchment. 'Go back to your roots!' To which he had replied, 'I have none.' At which she had retorted, 'Of course you don't! But grow some and be quick about it!' When he had continued to look helpless she had grown exasperated. 'Do what you say you do but don't: go down to your constituency and consult your people, your White Hart regulars... tomorrow!'

So it was that in the back parlour of the White Hart a private meeting of the best part of the committee of the Thanet Channel Constituency Labour Party was in session. There was an air of celebration in the room for had not their smart, dynamic MP become a member of the Shadow Cabinet? And was it not a racing certainty that in the forthcoming general election Labour would be swept to power? When that came to pass a member of the government would be representing them in Parliament. What gifts would he then be able to bestow on the constituency! The members of the committee were jubilant, certain that their confidence in their MP was soon to be well rewarded.

Lancing was touched, felt almost humbled by their enthusiasm. His mood was subdued. The theme for their meeting, he explained, was 'renewal'. He acknowledged his predicament, felt able to confide in those present. 'I have been promoted, but I feel at a loss. My staff have gone. I need to start again. I've been advised to get back to my roots and you are the very best of what I have. It was perhaps a little foolhardy of me to have relied so much on Westminster and those drawn to serve there. Now it is *you*, the grassroots, that must put me on the right track. I have my duties to Higher Education, of course, but what of the wider political agenda? What should my guiding principle be as I represent you in the coming Labour government?'

The members of his audience look at one another hesitantly, wondering whether their thoughts were heading in the same direction. All considered themselves Labour through and through so each, individually, they concluded, must have the same thought.

'You've always been popular in the constituency, Marcus. Never a bad word, that graffiti aside,' said Mr Foreshore, who taught geography at the constituency's largest comprehensive. 'You should do more of the same.'

'Yeah! And those people in Westminster have lost the plot,' added Tom Tudor, the local representative of the Environment Agency. 'If you want to stay on the right track you must stick to your principles and make sure you listen to your constituents. They want popular measures that make their lives that little bit better because what is popular with people is always what is in their best interests.'

'Yes, and taking care of the planet,' added district nurse Miriam Dreadfold.

'Right,' said Lancing, a gleam in his eye. 'Popular... populist... Isn't that populism?'

There was an uncomfortable silence until Mr Foreshore was bold enough to speak up. 'No, not populism, *popularism!*'

'Yes, what we need is *popularism!*' agreed Bill Ashford, the only Labour activist estate agent south of the Wash.

'*Yes, popularism!*' cried all, It was the evening's prize for collective thought, a strong, simple message: '*Popularism!*'

Several beers later Lancing came away from the meeting with his sense of purpose renewed. Popularism he could do! Out with 'disinterestedness' and in with 'popularism'! He would take on Jeff Deal's team and mould them to this, his new image. In the driveway of his constituency home he took a deep breath of *Parfum Brises de Mer*. He felt it was great to be alive. Could it, he wondered, be St Crispin's day?

FORTY-FIVE

The academic year was winding down but Conquest was busy. His book, *A Plan For The New University: A Vision For Higher Education Fit For Today And Tomorrow*, had finally been delivered by the printers. His publisher had arranged a book launch at the Royal Overseas League. Several vice-chancellors travelled considerable distances to be there. The Times Higher Education undertook to do a major feature. Conquest was pleased; the auspices were good. Marcus Lancing was invited to the reception but failed to attend. Conquest assumed he was much preoccupied by his new responsibilities as a member of the Shadow Cabinet, and sent him a copy of the book. A brief note of thanks came by return. A couple of weeks later he received a notification of a press briefing. The new Shadow Secretary of State for Higher Education was to make his inaugural public pronouncement. The staff from Lancing's office called Erma Radisch several times, urging her to ensure Conquest was present. Anticipation was high. The wise ancients sunning themselves on the River Terrace had noticed that Jeff Deal's staff had been unusually busy since Lancing had taken them on.

'Surely, he's going to put his foot in it?' they agreed with hoary glee.

The less pernicious hoped Lancing might announce a small but symbolic initiative suitable for inclusion in the manifesto of a reforming Labour government-in-waiting.

Conquest was there early; the Westminster conference hall still largely empty. He was surprised by how theatrical the set-up was. The hall was large and in semi-darkness, the podium brightly lit and backed by a huge projected graphic that read "Labour: Envisioning Empowermentation For Hard-Working Families". He took a seat in a side row, towards the back. He hadn't been there long before he heard an exclamation of pleasure and looked up to see the Re-Introductionist Tory MP, Clive Winston, sidling along the row towards him. Conquest had been inclined to dismiss Winston's Hermetic Conviction Narrative about Chinese intentions when first he had heard it, but now his feeling that there might well be some substance to it alternated with a helpless sense of being ill-informed. He felt awkward, half rose to his feet and held out his hand. Winston sat down besides him and surveyed the scene.

'Glad to catch up with you before this hoo-ha kicks off. Got a chap called Golding wants to meet you. He's the chair of the constituency committee in your old stamping ground.'

'I'm sorry?'

'*Golding.* You taught him in the days when you were still teaching. American Studies wasn't it? He was telling me he has a copy of your book on the Kennedys.'

Conquest was mystified for a moment longer, but his memory for names didn't fail him. 'Do you mean Richard Golding?'

The other nodded.

'Good Lord, yes, I remember him! He's in politics, is he?'

'Well, busy man. Good chair, independently minded. Thinks you'd be a perfect fit.'

'For what?'

It's that offer I mentioned to you, isn't it? Twenty thousand majority, incumbent just announced he's not standing again. We want to head off the One Nation flip-floppers. It's in his gift, Golding says, and I do believe him. How about it?'

Conquest shrugged warily. 'I'm rather caught off-guard!'

'Unless things change drastically Lancing's going to inherit the mess universities are in now. Look—' he delved into his briefcase and produced a copy of, *A Plan For The New University: A Vision For Higher Education Fit For Today And Tomorrow* – 'this is going to be required reading for us politicos, even the ones that don't read. When we're in opposition, as surely we will be, we see your book as a viable basis for what we should be promoting for our universities. You'll run rings round him; he hasn't a clue! It'll be your opportunity to shine and you might do some real good. Golding's going to be in town next week. The test match at Lord's: Aussies, first day. Join us for lunch, no obligation. I think you want it, and we can make it happen!'

Winston winked, slapped Conquest on the knee and prepared to leave. 'I'll send you the details.'

'You have my email address?'

'Of course!' He smiled broadly and off he went, making his way across the hall. Conquest sat back preoccupied by his thoughts. The hall was becoming noisily busy. Winston, he noticed, was heading for a figure on the further side of the podium with the look of the impresario about him, keeping an eye on his production from the shadow of the wings. It was the weirdly youthful Alex Slocum, the Senior Future Officer of Scribbling Inc. Winston spoke to him briefly, hand over his mouth as if he was aware he was within range of cameras. Conquest was pretty sure Slocum glanced in his direction. He now realised he detected Slocum's hand in the slogan behind the podium. Since Lancing's elevation he had heard no more from the boy wonder or Scribbling Inc. Had Clive Winston and the other Re-Introductionists been working in concert with Scribbling Inc to stop the University of the Wealds and Wolds? He wouldn't be surprised. Had Slocum, he wondered – more of a sinister idea, this – also had a hand in what Lancing was about to announce?

The hall was now full to overflowing. News of Lancing's maiden statement had clearly provoked an unusual amount of interest. The Press was there in force and many had come from both Houses, curious to see what he was going to say. By the time Lancing strode onto the stage, accompanied by several assistants carrying stacks of documents, the anticipation was palpable. An expectant hush fell on his audience. Dutifully, he kicked off with some endearing platitudes before he got down to the meat of his statement.

'As part of Labour's commitment to levelling up, I am today announcing our intention to support the creation of a new university in East Kent modelled on the University of the Highlands and Islands.'

Conquest stiffened. He felt like something small and harmless caught in a trap.

'We who have the care of East Kent in our hands share a concern that the region is notably underserved by institutions of Higher Education. There is a great deal of evidence that this has a detrimental effect on our communities, encouraging the movement of young people away from the area. To address the problem we are proposing the creation of a new university: the University of the Cinque Ports.'

There was a gentle ground swell of approval from the audience.

'The campus will be a collaboration between the historic towns known since time immemorial as the Cinque Ports – Sandwich, Dover, Hythe, New Romney and Hastings. At the end of this news conference we will be distributing copies of the environmental impact study prepared with the assistance of our Strategic Thinking Partner, Scribbling Inc. In it you will find projections for high quality jobs, population retention – even growth – brownfield accommodation units and new community facilities. In keeping with Labour's green pledges, Environmental Studies will be a particular focus of the new university, and in that connection we are pleased to announce a major, long-term sponsorship deal...'

Conquest could stand no more. He rose to his feet and, as inconspicuously as possible, worked his way towards the exit.

'...the China Investment Company...'

At the side entrance a knot of grave men – elderly, statesman-like – were standing, semi-incognito, there to pass judgment on Lancing's performance. As Conquest passed behind them, reaching for the door, one turned to greet him. It was Lord N'Garbi.

'Dear chap, making for the exit?' he exclaimed, easing through the door with him. 'Glad I caught you; I was told you'd be here. Lancing at full throttle, eh? Listen..." He grew confiding and drew Conquest to one side of the lobby. 'That constituency we were talking about. The constituency committee's chair is in London next week for Wimbledon. Wants to meet. Lawn tennis fan? We'll have lunch in the members' room; I'll arrange it. He thinks you're exactly what his constituency needs.'

Conquest's instinctive desire to escape had subsided. He laughed a bemused laugh. 'You know what I think in situations like this?'

'No, what do you think?'

'I think...perchance 'tis a game of two halves, *"press the re-start button"*!'

This book is printed on paper from sustainable sources managed under the Forest Stewardship Council (FSC) scheme.

It has been printed in the UK to reduce transportation miles and their impact upon the environment.

For every new title that Troubador publishes, we plant a tree to offset CO_2, partnering with the More Trees scheme.

For more about how Troubador offsets its environmental impact, see www.troubador.co.uk/sustainability-and-community